Wide Awake

Wide Awake

A Novel

Robert Bober

Translated from the French
by Carol Volk

The New Press gratefully acknowledges the Florence Gould
Foundation for supporting publication of this book.

The original title of this book, *On ne peut plus dormir tranquille quand on a une
fois ouvert les yeux*, was taken from "Plupart du temps" by Pierre Reverdy.

Originally published in France as *On ne peut plus dormir tranquille
quand on a une fois ouvert les yeux* by Editions P.O.L., Paris, 2010
Published in the United States by The New Press, New York, 2012
Distributed by Perseus Distribution

LIBRARY OF CONGRESS CATALOGING-IN-PUBLICATION DATA
Bober, Robert.
[On ne peut plus dormir tranquille quand on a une fois ouvert les yeux. English]
Wide awake : a novel / Robert Bober ; translated from the French by Carol Volk.
    p.   cm.
ISBN 978-1-59558-701-5 (pbk. : alk. paper)
    I. Volk, Carol.   II. Title.
    PQ2662.O243O513 2012
843'.914—dc23   2011033970

www.thenewpress.com

Composition by dix!
This book was set in Centaur MT

Printed in the United States of America

2   4   6   8   10   9   7   5   3   1

For Joachim and for Sacha
For Henri

I was only twenty, but my memory preceded my birth.

—Patrick Modiano,
Livret de famille

Wide Awake

PROLOGUE

While I prefer buses to trains—and I always choose a spot standing in the back on the open deck—I still like walking best. I love getting lost in the sites, and ignoring the shortcuts home.

I live in Paris, in the XIth arrondissement. At 7 Rue Oberkampf, with my mother and my little brother Alex. Just the three of us. My father died when I was two years old. In July 1942. Or thereabout, we don't know exactly. He died just as Gad Wolf died, who lived at number 8, just as the Polkowska family died, who lived at number 18, just as the Kistalkas died from number 38, the Wargas from 13, and the Dodineks from 16. I know them by name from hearing my mother mention them so often. The names always followed by the address, each time. So as not to forget.

That's about all I know about them. I know a bit more about my father, but to describe him I need to look at his picture. We have one, in a brown leather frame, sitting on the sideboard of the dining room. But as with all photographs that sit in the very same spot, without variation, over time you stop seeing them.

• • •

My mother rarely speaks about her childhood. She says little about the time before my birth, about the dreams she shared with my father. Just a name, sometimes, or a date.

My parents were born in Przytyk, a town in Poland not far from the city of Radom, the population of which was mostly Jewish. I think they met during a protest that had followed a pogrom led by Polish fascists. Several people died and more than a hundred were wounded. It was March 9, 1936. My mother was nineteen, my father twenty-one. They got married the next year.

My mother had already lost her father. Born Hannah Horovitz, she became Hannah Appelbaum. Shortly afterward, at my father's insistence, they left Poland to come live in France, where they were soon joined by my maternal grandmother, whom my mother didn't want to leave alone.

My mother was an only child, which was very rare at the time. Not long ago I learned that before my mother was born, my grandmother—whom I called Bubbe and who died last year—had had a first child. A boy who died very young from some sort of illness, exactly what sort I don't remember.

When they arrived in France, my father, whose name was Yankel, called himself Jacques. My mother kept her first name.

After living for some time in a small hotel at Passage Kuszner, my parents moved to 7 Rue Oberkampf, in an area called the Cité Crussol, close to the Cirque d'Hiver or Winter Circus. A carpenter or woodworker, I don't recall which, had worked within this complex of courtyards and alleys for a long time, and whenever I go there I picture myself as a little boy. He would receive deliveries of entire trees cut into planks, and we children would play on top of them, despite the many warnings we received. Maybe it wasn't chance but the small-town nature of this artisan-filled neighborhood that had led my parents, who had just arrived from their village in Poland, to live there in the first place. At least that's what I like to think.

I was born on May 2, 1940. My mother had wanted to call me Joseph, after her father, Yossel Berish, but the war was already on and it had seemed wise to give me a name like Bernard instead.

My father was taken away in July 1942, a few days after the great raid of the Vel d'Hiv, in circumstances that I'll come back to later.

Until then he had been working as a top piece cutter for a shoe manufacturer on the Rue Julien-Lacroix. We still have a leather-cutting knife at home which my mother kept. I use it to sharpen my pencils.

In 1946, during a charity event organized at the Intercontinental Hotel by the Union of Jewish Organizations in France, my mother encountered a childhood friend, Leizer, who was also from her home town of Przytyk, and who had survived Auschwitz. After many long months of wandering from one displaced persons' camp to another, he had ended up in Paris. As an experienced tailor, he easily found a spot as a mechanic in a women's clothing manufacturer on the Rue de Turenne. It's strange that my mother took this street every day to go to work on the Rue des Francs-Bourgeois where she was a saleswoman in an antique jewelry store, yet they had never run into one another before.

One year later, Alex was born, my half brother. In 1949, Leizer, who became my stepfather, decided to go visit his sister, who had left Poland for New York as a teenager with the hope of becoming a music hall dancer. His plane crashed near the Azores. There were no survivors. That was twelve years ago.

As a result, I don't remember my own father, but I do remember my brother's father, while my brother does not.

I roam about my past, here and there gathering tiny bits and pieces, attempting to reconstruct them, as if one could exist another time . . .

—Henri Calet,
Le tout sur le tout

I

Thanks to Robert, whom I ran into about three months ago, I am going to be an extra in a film by François Truffaut.

I was heading home from a friend's house on the Rue de Belleville when I happened upon him. Despite the fact that his hands and a camera were covering part of his face, I recognized him right away. He turned to me in amazement as soon as I called his name. And as if my name popped into his head as he was scrutinizing my face, he articulated it very deliberately.

"Bernard Appelbaum?"

And after mutual smiles,

"Tarnos 1953? . . . or 1954?"

It was both, in fact. Robert had been my counselor at a summer camp in Tarnos, in the Landes region of France. In 1953, and again in 1954. I hadn't seen him since. We had lost track of one another. That was almost seven years ago.

After a few banalities—"What are you doing here? Do you live in the neighborhood?"—we almost said good-bye without learning anything more about one other. But then, while he was taking some pictures through the gate of the Villa Ottoz where we were standing, Robert suggested I come along with him.

He still had some pictures to take at the Villa Castel, he told me, and explained as we were walking that François Truffaut was getting ready to make a film which was set mainly before World War I, and had asked him to take some pictures of potential locations. The film didn't really take place in Belleville, but Robert, who had become Truffaut's assistant, explained that this neighborhood still had many sites that looked exactly as they had fifty years before. Truffaut had wanted to film in Montmartre where he grew up, Robert told me, reminding me that several scenes in *The 400 Blows* had been filmed there. Yet because Montmartre had been in so many films, Robert thought it had come to look like a film set, and had suggested that Truffaut consider Belleville. Which was why he was photographing the neighborhood that day.

As I was listening to Robert, my mind went back several years to the days when he was my camp counselor. I seemed to recall that he had been a tailor at the time, and I wondered how he had come to work with Truffaut. But I didn't dare ask.

While we were talking, and as if to keep his distance from our conversation, Robert was taking photos of the Villa Castel, the narrow passage with a tiled floor that led to a private garden on the Rue des Couronnes. He also took a picture of a cat that was looking at us, but just for fun it seemed.

A little later, we sat down at a small café on the Rue des Envierges, the owner of which, Nadine, shook hands with us. Robert ordered a coffee and I ordered a hot chocolate.

On the table, he put down his camera—an Agfa—and in a

small notebook with stars on the cover made a list of the places he had just photographed, noting very precisely the place and time of each shot.

"Once the pictures are developed," he explained, "I show them to Truffaut. Then he chooses the ones that interest him and we visit the locations together."

"Is that always how it's done?"

My questions were obviously naive, which may explain why I remember that day in such detail.

That's when I remember learning that Robert had grown up on the Rue de Rébéval, on the other side of the Rue de Belleville, and that when I met him taking pictures of the Villa Ottoz, he had just seen a little house that had struck him as exactly what Truffaut was looking for, a house inhabited by a painter, Pierre Alechinsky—I remember Robert laughing because I had understood him to say Alex Chinsky. But because the painter's house was filled with canvases, Robert had found an alternative next door.

Behind the bar in Nadine's bistro was a partition, the top of which was made of etched glass, that separated the room we were in from another, smaller room, generally reserved for eating. Because Nadine made home-cooked meals, but only for lunch, for a few regulars. Despite the lateness of the hour, it seemed we could still hear the clanking of forks. I've since learned from personal experience that at Nadine's you hang around even after you're done eating.

Out of that room came a man, the kind you notice right away. He wore a thick brown corduroy suit, a yellow flannel shirt, a red knit tie, and in his breast pocket where you sometimes put a hand-kerchief was the bowl of a pipe. He had a little goatee, and hardly any hair on his head.

He was coming toward us with a smile that grew when Robert noticed him and stood to greet him.

I stood as well, feeling intimidated. Robert gestured toward him and introduced him as Anatole Jakowsky.

They exchanged a few words, by which I realized that the man knew about Robert's quest. After paying his check with Nadine, his hand already on the door handle, he turned to us again.

"Ask Nadine for the key to the basement. You'll see a master-piece of urban naive painting."

And he left.

"He's an amazing character," Robert told me, "one of the great-est specialists on naive painting. But not only that. He also has a ton of collections: pipes, postcards, particularly of the First World War, and of bicycles."

"How did you meet him?"

"Through bicycles, actually. Someone told me about a vintage bike dealer at the Saint-Ouen flea market. I went there because we needed some for the film. I was told to go see him because he knows a lot about bicycles. The dealer gave me his telephone num-ber, and that's how we met. His advice is invaluable. For example, he taught me that before the war, almost all men wore mustaches, and that during the war most of them shaved them off. It's a good way to show the passage of time. In fact, if you'd like, we'll need extras for an important scene in a bistro. You could see how we shoot. What do you think? . . . Jeanne Moreau will be there."

"Well . . . I'd like that. What do I need to do?"

"Nothing. You'll be sitting at a table and drinking a drink, just like you're doing now. But it's not until the end of April, or beginning of May. The leaves will be on the trees. . . . Anyway, to get back to Jakowsky, the fact that neither of us was born in France certainly helped us connect. He was born in Romania, in Kishinev, where there was a pogrom in 1905. Part of the film takes place in Germany too, and he told me that before the war he had a plan to tour Germany by bicycle. But, hearing about the persecution the Jews were starting to suffer, he abandoned his plan out of solidarity. . . . Hey, finish your hot chocolate, if it isn't too cold," continued Robert after a silence, "we'll ask Nadine for the key to the basement to see the painting he was talking about."

The painting Anatole Jakowsky had referred to was painted directly on the wall. All the corridors of the basement were painted, transformed into neighborhood streets. Street signs, which were also painted, gave the names: Rue des Couronnes, Rue de Belleville, Rue Piat, Rue des Envierges of course, since that's the street we were on, the Rue Vilin with its stairway and footbridge over the station of the Little Belt train. The painter had reconstituted a piece of his town with everything it needed—gas lamps and lopsided houses beneath a clear, blue sky. He had also painted the house that was filmed in *Casque d'Or* and pasted a picture of Simone Signoret cut from a magazine on it. On a piece of stone wall that jutted into the basement, he had also pasted the remains of a poster announcing a protest in front of the "Communards' Wall" in honor of the martyrs of the Paris Commune. Next to it was Nadine's bistro, with an actual bottle crate on the floor.

But while this immense fresco was resonant with the painter's memories, there was a strange absence of human beings in this tangle of streets and alleys. No one was walking, there were no concierges on their doorsteps, no children were playing bocce ball or hopscotch, there wasn't even a cat or a dog. Only some musical notes were floating from the window of a house on the Rue Botha in which Maurice Chevalier was born, above which was written one of his songs:

The boys of Ménilmontant
Are always ascending
Even while redescending
The streets of Ménilmuche . . .

This painting, which was probably meant to bear witness to the neighborhood as it was, showed signs of a few worrisome repairs. And you could imagine the artist intent on keeping the signs of dampness at bay with continual efforts at restoration.

"It was painted by a retiree who lives in the building," Nadine told us when Robert gave her back the key. "He started over two years ago and he still comes back almost every day. At times I wonder why he keeps coming back now that he's done. Sometimes I go down to get some bottles and I see him sitting there on his folding chair, staring . . . as if he's keeping watch over the streets."

"Doesn't it bother him, all that paint chipping off the damp walls?" asked Robert.

"Well, not really," replied Nadine, "because he doesn't get along very well with his wife, so to get away from the fighting, he takes his paint, his brushes, and his chair and he goes 'to the picture,' as he likes to say. For him, the 'picture' is what's in his head. It's not far to go. I don't know if the arguments prompt him to come down three flights or if, on the contrary, it's the touch-ups on his painting that draw him out of the house, but he's a happy camper. When he's finished, he takes a little break with a glass of muscatel, and then he goes back upstairs with his supplies and his chair and turns on the TV. Monsieur Jakowsky loves the painting, but he calls it 'a vain attempt to hold back time.' That's his expression. It's true that you wonder who will touch it up when Monsieur Fernand isn't around anymore to work on it."

We stopped at a big grassy strip less than a hundred meters from Chez Nadine, on which two apartment buildings had been erected. Situated at the corner of the Rue Piat, the Rue des Envierges, and the Rue du Transvaal, overlooking the stairs of the Rue Vilin, it seemed to have been conceived as a perch over the most beautiful panorama of the city.

"Have you seen the film *Casque d'Or?*" Robert asked.

"With Simone Signoret? Yes, I've seen it, but a long time ago."

"Well, this is it. This is the spot where Jacques Becker shot several scenes."

And Robert showed me the wood shop where Serge Reggiani worked, the bakery in front of which Simone Signoret had her carriage wait. He talked about the smack she gave Reggiani on the very spot where we were standing. He remembered the exact line: "Beg your pardon, but I got it yesterday. Now we're even."

"I'd love for Truffaut to shoot some scenes here too," he added, "because it's nice when films hark back to their antecedents."

I felt like I was seeing what he was seeing before seeing it for myself. On this spot where a few remnants of the past subsisted, these memories seemed to find a home in Robert. And in listening to him speak so passionately about *Casque d'Or*, I could picture him again at the summer camp, at night in our rooms, talking to us about the films he loved.

"You need to come here early in the morning, when the sun is rising behind us, in March or April," continued Robert. "You buy a chocolate croissant at the bakery on the corner, you lean on the balcony, and you watch. People aren't talking too loudly yet, there are only a few workers on their way to work, heading for the Couronnes metro, and you've got the beauty of Paris awakening before you."

We grew silent as we gazed at Paris, silhouetted against the late afternoon winter sky. Below, on the Boulevard de Belleville, a police siren broke the silence.

Then Robert gave me his telephone number and address. He didn't live far from me, on the Rue Mesley, on the other side of the Place de la République. We shook hands. He wanted to return to the bistro he'd mentioned, the one where they would need extras. I promised to call him and we each went our own way. He headed back up the Rue Piat to see the bistro by night, having seen it only by day, while I descended the stairs of the Rue Vilin to head home.

2

Robert had found the bistro behind the Place des Fêtes. On a dead-end street, Impasse Compans.

A sign on the gate read: "Chez Victor, café, bocce ball." Once past the gate, you found yourself in a kind of farmyard, at the rear of which, accessible via an open-work staircase, was a platform or stage on legs, surrounded by a railing, the kind that still exists in open-air country dances, where the orchestras perch.

From there, below us, as far as the eye could see, lay the communes of Lilas and Pre-Saint-Gervais with their village houses, interspersed with groves and vegetable gardens.

It was to this peaceful-looking haven, more like an outdoor dance hall than a bistro, that I went to be in a movie, and I couldn't get over it.

It wasn't ten o'clock yet and I didn't know where to go. I was trying to take in everything that was going on, most of it incomprehensible to me.

"He must be inside," someone who was moving a gas lamp told me when I asked where I could find Robert.

You entered Chez Victor by descending three steps and passing

ROBERT BOBER

Les Films du Carrosse   Film : Jules et Jim
Tél : BAL 48 61
                        Journée du Mardi 2 Mai 1961
                           18è jour de tournage
                           Horaire : 12h - 19h30

Lieu de tournage : Café Victor - Tél : BOT 14 - 99
                   Impasse Compans (métro Place des fêtes)
Décor :   Intérieur Caf'Conc
                   Extérieur Caf'Conc
Scènes à tourner : Nuit - 7
                   Jour - 91

Acteurs	Rôles	Costumes	Maquillage	Prêts à Tourner
Oscar WERNER	Jules	prévu	11h30	12
Henri SERRE	Jim	prévu	11h30	12
Marie DUBOIS	Thérèse	prévu	11 h	12 h
Pierre FABRE	l'homme saoul	prévu	11h30	12 h
Figuration : 8 hommes - 8 femmes			10 h	12 h

Accessoires : Photos Gertrude, Lucie, Birgitta, tables
              rondes couleur sombre - Cigares - piano
              mécanique - cendriers époque - accessoires
              décor café d'époque 1914 - rideaux époque -
              lustres gaz - becs de gaz mobiles - papier
              à lettres - écritoires -verres et tasses
              d'époque.

Electriciens équipement 8 h Café Victor - Impasse Compans
             (rue Compans) Métro : Place des Fêtes -
             1h arrêt pour déjeuner - prêt 11h

Machinistes : 8 h rue Piat - chargement matériel - prévoir
              Borniol pour installation chez Victor (prêt
              pour midi) 1h arrêt pour déjeuner.

200 Kgs REMY 8 h rue Piat - chargement des pannières
              costumes figuration et accessoires Caf'Conc
              Disposition de M.CAPEL pour aménagement du
              décor Caf'Conc.

1 coiffeuse supplémentaire -   10 H sur place.

Habilleuse - Maquilleuse :   10 H sur place.

Accessoiriste : 9 H sur place - 1 h arrêt déjeuner.

16

through a double glass door which was wide open and which led to a first room with two posters on the walls, one announcing a dance at the Moulin de la Galette, the other advertising a painting exhibition by Picasso at Ambroise Vollard's gallery. In a second room with a stovepipe running through it was the bar, and there was another room where young women whom I imagined to be extras were having their hair done.

"Here's Bernard," said Robert, as if someone else knew me besides him.

Someone else did know me in fact; she was just finishing having her hair done and she turned around. My heart leapt: it was Laura. Laura with whom I'd been in love seven years earlier when we had been together at the summer camp at Tarnos, where Robert had been our counselor.

I hadn't seen her since, and yet the feelings I'd had for her remained strangely intact.

On hikes, we'd walk close to one another, synchronizing our steps. I swam at her side. And that was the extent of it. I was fourteen and that was enough for me. It was enough for me to know that she offered nothing more to others. That she preferred no one else.

I knew that Laura, like many of those who were at the camp, didn't remember her deported parents. She had always lived in a home for orphaned children. And stupidly, I couldn't help being jealous of those who had shared her life for those years.

She told me one day—shortly before the camp ended, with emotion in her voice—that she was tired of eating every day in a mess hall, of sleeping every night in a dormitory, of reading only books from the library, and many other things that she would have liked to do alone. I understood her pain and would have liked to kiss her, to hug her, but I didn't dare move, knowing that a gesture of tenderness would have brought on tears.

That very afternoon, however, I had taken her hand and we'd run on the beach all the way to the water. Then, giving herself to the waves, Laura began to laugh and nothing more was said.

Now here was Laura, less pale than she was at thirteen, smiling at my surprise.

"Happy birthday, Bernard."

Happy birthday? How could she have remembered? Did Robert tell her? And how would he have known? In questioning him with my eyes, I realized that he had grown a mustache, following Jakowsky's advice.

"Come, we'll pick out a costume for you," he said without even mentioning the birthday.

Ten minutes later, I was dressed in a black cotton vest buttoned up to the neck and a baggy pair of thick brown corduroy trousers that narrowed at the ankles, like carpenters wore.

"You know, I think you're wearing Reggiani's pants," said Robert pleasantly, referring to Serge Reggiani, who had played the carpenter in *Casque d'or*. "And while I think of it, don't forget to take off your wristwatch before the filming starts."

As the set was being arranged, I went to join Laura, who was waiting, leaning on the railing of the little stage. Of course we didn't mention our common memories. Others, broken with silence, snaked randomly through the seven intervening years.

Laura informed me that she was working at Brentano's, an Anglo-American bookstore on the Avenue de l'Opéra, where she'd been hired because of her knowledge of English. She had learned English during a long stay with an English family that had wanted to adopt her. Although she'd been touched, Laura had declined, but maintained good relations with the family, visiting them from time to time.

She went on: "As for Robert, I had also lost touch with him, just as you had. And then one day, almost a year ago, he showed up at Brentano's, not knowing that I worked there. He was asking for the American edition of a noir thriller: *Shoot the Piano Player* by David Goodis, also known as *Down There*. That's how we found one another, and that's also how I learned that he'd begun working with François Truffaut. We've seen each other two or three times since. The last time was shortly after you two met, and he asked me to be an extra in this film. That's how I knew you'd be here today. Since it was a Tuesday, when the bookstore isn't too crowded, I was able to get the day off easily."

It had been decided that, for the scene in which we were needed, Laura and I would be seated at the same table. It was for a scene in a series called "7."

The action was decided before the extras were in place: the camera was loaded onto tracks and would follow Jim, played by Henri Serre, across one of the rooms of the café.

"You're in love" was the only direction Robert gave us, when Truffaut asked for a rehearsal. Laura and I looked at each other. She smiled, and casually placed her hands in mine.

I was too overwhelmed to understand what was happening around our table. While I was holding Laura's hands, Truffaut came toward us:

"Did Robert tell you? You should be kissing when the camera passes in front of you."

Had Robert told Truffaut who we were?

The clapper board snapped, and the camera, moving silently on its tracks, came toward us, pointed at us, and continued on, following Henri Serre. Three times. Three times, when the camera passed, I put my lips to Laura's, and these three kisses instantly revived what I had thought lost, yet which seven years had not erased. Thank you, François Truffaut. Each time Truffaut yelled, "Cut!" Laura was the first to pull her lips from mine. After the third time, it was over. Everyone was already preparing for the next scene, which would be shot outside the bistro. I gazed at Laura's hands, which I didn't dare reach for again.

3

Since it was expected that I would return the next day, Robert gave me a copy of the schedule as he was distributing them to the other members of the film crew.

I kept it on me, carefully folded in my pocket, and in the alley, as soon as I exited through the gate of Chez Victor, I read it again, as if trying to learn it by heart. Which I did:

Film: *Jules and Jim.* May 3, 1961. 19th day of filming. 9:00 AM– 18:00 PM. Location: Café Victor, Impasse Compans. Metro: Place des Fêtes. Telephone: BOT.14.99. And then, the number of scenes to be shot and the names of the actors. Only Jeanne Moreau had to be called on to appear. For the others, it was the same as for the extras: nine hours on standby, ready to shoot. That's what I had done, even though Robert had told me he would only need me in the afternoon. But whereas the day before I had focused on the three kisses with Laura, I was now interested in seeing how the filming worked.

There was an actor there speaking with Truffaut who wasn't listed on the schedule, and whom I recognized from having heard him sing songs by Aristide Bruant at Chez Moineau, a cabaret on the Rue Guenegaud.

As soon as he saw me, Robert asked if I felt capable of driving a three-wheeled delivery cart. Seeing my hesitation, he decided it was wiser to dress in me a big unbleached painter's smock. "You'll walk in front of the café this afternoon, carrying a housepainter's ladder on your shoulder."

It wasn't long before I realized how fortunate my hesitation had been. One of the technicians, as it turned out, had just straddled the three-wheeled cart, and, leaning to the wrong side on a turn, had caused it to tip over, falling along with it. A fall that caused the entire crew to burst out laughing, including Truffaut, who I had thought, perhaps naively, wouldn't laugh out loud. That could have been me.

As foreseen on the schedule, a 1914 touring car pulled up outside the gate, followed by a "1914 delivery truck."

I watched the comings and goings from the stage—the platform on which, a short time ago, I had spent so much time with Laura. Near me, an extra was reading *The Social War*, an anarchist daily which had been a prop on the set the day before. The headline read TO HELL WITH THEM, I SAY.

I myself ended up having time to read this newspaper, because it was only in the late afternoon that I was called on to walk in front of the café, as Robert had requested, a ladder resting on my shoulder.

In this scene, which Truffaut called "Catherine and Jim miss their appointment" but was referred to as "38H" on the clapper board, the camera was placed inside the bistro in the direction of what was supposed to be the street. And at the moment that

Jeanne Moreau would descend the three steps, I was supposed to walk by with my ladder in the other direction, passing the horse-drawn delivery cart. After which, as Jeanne Moreau left the bistro disappointed, the "touring car" would pass, followed by the infamous three-wheeled cart. Everything having been perfectly orchestrated, there were only two takes.

I returned to this bistro where, thanks to Robert, I had been re-acquainted with Laura. I went back there to meet with her again. When I had asked for her address, she had told me to call her at Brentano's: "It's easiest to reach me at the bookstore. I'm there every day, Tuesday to Saturday." By phone, we agreed to meet on Monday, May 22, and I had thought it was a good idea to meet at Chez Victor, where we had played lovers.

I arrived early, and without the film crew the place seemed different. A plant which had taken root at the foot of the front gate, and which during the filming I hadn't noticed, stretched against the wall. The gramophone and posters announcing the Picasso exhibit and the Moulin de la Galette event were gone. Tables and chairs had been placed on the stage, some of which were occupied by bocce ball players. "They're from Piedmont," Monsieur Victor, the owner, told me some time later. "They come almost every day. Only men." They had taken a break from their game to drink a beer. But I didn't mind their presence. Thanks to the beautiful weather, it was empty inside the café, and I was happy to be able to sit at the table where I had held Laura's hands in mine.

No one was passing with a ladder on his shoulder when, like Jeanne Moreau, Laura descended the three steps leading into the café. We smiled. I, at the memory of Jeanne Moreau, she, because I had chosen the same table, as she had expected.

She kissed me on the cheek in a friendly way and ordered a grenadine, as I had done.

The cautious kiss should have been a warning to me. I had so anticipated this moment that it didn't sink in. Seated at this bistro table, so close to Laura, on this almost summer day, I could feel her aura, as in those moments together at summer camp, and this strange, almost mysterious thing troubled me too much for me to understand that it was love. Despite all those years when we hadn't seen one another, those moments had left their imprint and had been revived when I held her hand and kissed her at Truffaut's behest.

Our conversation began with the silence I had feared ever since we had made this date, and which Laura attempted to fill by taking tiny sips of her grenadine. Meanwhile, I wondered if the kisses—those kisses I dared not seek to replicate on her lips—had been the prelude to a story of an importance that neither Truffaut nor Robert had suspected.

We spoke about Robert.

Did she know how he had gotten into film? Yes, she did.

"When I saw him we had lunch at a restaurant near the bookstore. I remembered, as you did, that back when he was a camp counselor he had been working as a tailor, so I asked him how he had gotten into film. Because I knew that loving film wasn't enough to become Truffaut's assistant. By then he wasn't a tailor any more, he had worked at other jobs, like a potter. And I think he was working in an office at the time he contacted Truffaut. He had read in the newspaper—*France-Soir* I think it was, yes, it was

France-Soir, because he'd said: 'You see, there are no bad books, or newspapers'—so in *France-Soir* there was a classified saying that Truffaut was looking for children of about the age of thirteen, boys, to act in a movie. Robert wrote to him to see if he might need someone to take care of the children during the shoot. He didn't get a reply. Two weeks later, he decided to go see Truffaut, who agreed to see him and who remembered his letter. He hadn't taken the time to respond because he was in the middle of preparing for his film, and he didn't think he needed anyone because he already had assistants who could watch the children. Robert was a little disappointed but he was nonetheless glad to have had a chance to chat with Truffaut. He told him about the camp, the little shows he put on with us and all that. He was especially happy because just as he was leaving, Truffaut called him back and handed him a script. It was *The 400 Blows*. He told him, 'Read this, and if you don't mind, I'd like your opinion—the opinion of someone from outside the film world—and call me back to let me know what you think.' So, he wasn't exactly hired, but before he had even reached the stairs he began flipping the pages of the script to read it. They saw each other a few days later to talk about it. I don't remember what Robert told me about their conversation, except that they spoke about Jean Vigo's *Zero for Conduct*. That's right, at the time he was working in a big office, because a few weeks later, when the filming had already begun, one night Truffaut called him on the phone. He told him he had been right and that if he could come watch the children, it would be helpful. It was for all the school scenes. Because the children were messing around in the courtyard and each time there was a scene to shoot with one or two actors, the children would make so much noise it was ruining the sound. You can imagine how happy Robert was. He told Truffaut he couldn't come the next day because he needed a day to build up to being sick at work, but that he would be there the day after. Robert told me he wanted it to work out so much that he already had a fever when he arrived at work the next day. Just the sight of him caused his boss to tell him to go home and take care of himself, but Robert didn't want to seem suspicious so he told him that it was nothing, it would pass. When he didn't come to work the next day, no one was surprised, and meanwhile Robert was already on the set. He took the children to the school playground—there was an entire class of kids—and organized mime games and, you know, all those quiet games we played at camp at night. So Truffaut was able to shoot normally. The problem was that, since he was organizing the games, Robert couldn't watch the filming, even though he was dying to see how it worked. But he told me that there was a great moment that evening, after the first day of filming, when Truffaut told him, 'I'm very happy, that went well, and if you're interested, I'll take you to see the rushes we filmed yesterday.' Robert sat in the car next to Truffaut, who took him to see what he had filmed the day before, and at that moment he said he had the feeling that the film world was opening its arms to him. The other great moment was at the end of the filming, when Truffaut, who knew him a bit better by then, told him: 'I know you want to get into film, so if you'd like, I'll hire you as my assistant for my next film.' After he told me all that, Robert concluded by saying: 'And that's my fairy tale.' And Truffaut kept his word, because Robert worked on *Shoot the Piano Player*, the book he'd come to find at the bookstore, and now he's working on *Jules and Jim*."

• • •

The more I listened to Laura, the more I wondered why Robert had thought to reunite us for this shoot. When did he decide to ask us to play lovers? Did he know before the filming started? Or was it Truffaut who had asked him at the last minute?

Then I did as I had done the day of the filming, I took Laura's hands in mine. She didn't react. She just looked at me with a kind of sad benevolence and I understood that that was as far as things would go. That the kisses on the set, each time interrupted by Truffaut's "Cut," were just fake kisses, film kisses. That the feelings that had recklessly sprung up in me were bound to be quashed. I pulled my hands back.

"But you kissed me."

"Because Robert asked us to."

"No, it was Truffaut. Robert just asked us to be in love with one another."

"It's the same thing," replied Laura.

We were both equally uncomfortable with this conversation, and, as if to distract us, a cat leapt onto the zinc bar and stretched out, absorbing a little coolness.

We realized that the time had come to say good-bye, that Laura had to take the initiative, and do so carefully, knowing that in my confusion I would have been incapable of saying good-bye without being brusque.

"Let me go first," she said. She gave me the same kind of kiss she had when she arrived, and headed for the open door. Then she hesitated a moment, as if her body had moved too quickly, and stood before the three steps. Seeing perhaps that, overcome by sadness, I wasn't even trying to salvage anything, Laura came back and put her lips to mine. Then, signaling me not to move, know-ing I was watching her leave, she left without turning back.

This final kiss had the effect of increasing the distance between us, and this contradiction hardly surprised me.

Laura left behind a book of photographs on the table, a book she had given me when she arrived and which I hadn't opened yet. I could picture her hands placing the book in front of me. It was a book titled *The Family of Man*, the catalogue to a major exhibition organized by Edward Steichen at the Museum of Modern Art in New York.

I leafed through the book. Photographs from sixty-eight coun-tries were organized by themes, such as marriage, birth, mother and child, games, work, solitude, and family. It was the latter theme, family, that drew my attention. There was an Italian fam-ily, a South African family, a Japanese family, and another that grabbed me even more. It showed an American family of eleven, standing around an elderly relative seated on a little rocking chair. Perhaps at the photographer's request, or of their own volition, these eleven people were standing against a wall with four care-fully framed portraits of ancestors. Two men and two women. I realized why this photograph had caught my attention—it must have been taken at this specific spot in order to create an image in which they would all be together, the living and those who came before them.

The first sentence of the prologue, which I only briefly skimmed initially, said: "The first cry of a newborn baby in Chicago or Zamboango, in Amsterdam or Rangoon, has the same pitch and key, each saying, 'I am! I have come through! I belong! I am a member of the Family.' "

Little by little, I stopped being able to separate the images in this book from what Laura had said to me when she'd arrived. Like me, she had noticed the remnants of a recent fire on the street near Chez Victor, on the second story of a building. She made a remark to which I hadn't paid particular attention: "I hope they saved their photo album." That was it. And she ordered her grenadine.

As I leafed through this book of photographs, memories of the adolescent girl at the summer camp came to mind. I knew that something in her had been broken, then glued back together. But only glued.

I had learned that when she was just a little girl, in the orphanage, Laura had drawn wrinkles and put lipstick on her doll. She had made her doll into an adult. She had even been seen to place herself in the arms of her doll to see how it felt to be in the arms of a mother. *The Family of Man* album and her comment about the fire nearby reminded me of the doll's wrinkles.

And I then understood this book—which, before opening it, I couldn't help but take as a breakup gift, even though nothing had even gotten started—as the sign of a shared intimacy, like the final kiss whose meaning I hadn't understood. And I didn't even try to hold back my tears.

4

On Tuesday, January 24, 1962, *Jules and Jim* appeared on the screen, and that Friday night my mother and I went to see it at the Vendôme Theater, Avenue de l'Opéra. We went without Alex, because the film was restricted for those under eighteen, and he was only fourteen. He was furious, because a looming strike meant he wasn't even sure he'd be able to watch television.

My heart constricted at the thought of seeing Laura again. Those kisses we'd shared, now dormant, would be present again through the magic of film. And when, seated in the dark, before the film even started, I heard Jeanne Moreau's voice say, "You said: I love you / I said: wait / I was about to say: take me / You said: go," my heartsickness returned, as if it had simply gotten lost and had now found its home.

My mother rarely went to the movies. That night she was happy to be with me and excited to see me on the screen, however fleetingly. When I saw myself passing with the ladder on my shoulder, I barely had time to point myself out. Nonetheless, she smiled trustingly, even though my appearance was too short to recognize me. Impatiently, I awaited the other scene. I waited in vain: not a trace remained of what the camera had filmed of me and Laura. The scene where Jim talks to Florencie was there, but the scene before it, the only one that mattered to me, had been cut.

As soon as the lights went up, as I was helping my mother put on her coat, I had the urge to see the film again, quickly, as if something in me refused to let go of that moment of tenderness, a tenderness from which Laura was now definitively liberated by the absence of the scene in the film.

Why had the scene been filmed and then cut?

I didn't want to talk about it, but I had to say something to my mother. She smiled at me again, a little sadly this time, but had no consolation to offer.

She gave me her arm when we reached the street. I didn't recall her ever having done that before. And I wondered how long it had been since we'd gone to the movies together. Six years? Seven? Maybe more. "Let's get a hot drink," she said when we arrived at the Place de l'Opéra. In the café, when the waiter brought a hot chocolate for me and a tea for my mother, she reminded him to bring her the slice of lemon he'd forgotten and a glass. She always drank tea from a glass, cupping her hands around it.

Once we were warmed up, she suggested we walk part of the way home. We remained quiet another moment. Then she asked me if I had read the book on which the film was based. No, I hadn't read it. "I'd like to read it," she told me: and so began the story I would then learn about my parents.

The story of Jules, Jim, and Catherine—what Truffaut had called a pure three-way love affair—was like an echo of what my mother had lived. And as if the film had brought it all back to life, she started off by telling me about how she met my father and Leizer during the protests that followed the pogrom of Przytyk.

"Yankel and Leizer knew one another already. They both belonged to the same Jewish socialist organization: the Bund. They lived in the same neighborhood and had attended the same school. And then at fifteen, your father learned the shoe trade with his father, and Leizer learned that of tailor with his. After the protest, I also joined the Bund, while others signed up with the left-wing Zionists, with the Dror or with Hashomer. Since almost the entire population of Przytyk was Jewish, there was room for several organizations. After that, Yankel, Leizer, and I were inseparable. We went to political gatherings together and danced on Saturday nights. Sometimes we went to Radom, which was nearby and where good orchestras played modern music like tango or rumba. One day we found out that a big dance was being organized in Radom with an orchestra that had come especially from Warsaw, and we decided to go. On Saturday night, there was always a bus that went from Przytyk to Radom. The bus was scheduled to leave at seven, and you couldn't miss it because it was the last one that evening. We agreed that the three of us would meet shortly before the bus was to leave. But at seven o'clock, Leizer still wasn't there. We asked the driver to wait, telling him that our friend was just a little delayed, but since there were other passengers, he had to leave after waiting another fifteen minutes. We figured that Leizer had gotten tied up at the last minute and hadn't had time to tell us, so we went to the dance without him. Your father was a great tango dancer, you know. That night, I danced only with him, and when you dance all night with the same man, it's not like dancing with just another partner, who walks you back to your table and says thank you. It was on our way back from Radom that we kissed for the first time."

My mother, who had seemed shaken, clinging to my arm as we left the movie, regained a bit of calm as she spoke about the past when they were all three in Poland. Now she was quiet, as if lingering back in the time before the black hole.

"And Leizer," I asked her, "what had happened to him?"

"Leizer? . . . It's a silly story. I told you that he worked for his father, and that day he absolutely had to finish and deliver a suit for a wedding that was taking place the next day. So Saturday, while his father was giving the suit a final pressing, Leizer thought he would save time by dressing up in the suit he wore on big occasions—and the dance in Radom was that type of occasion. When he returned from the delivery, his mother put a bowl of soup on the kitchen table for him, because there was no way she was going to let him leave without a bowl of soup in his belly. But in his haste, and worried about being late, he made some movement and spilled the soup on his pant leg. A fatty soup, like they make in Poland, so you can imagine how the pants looked. He immediately rinsed them with hot water to clean them while his mother was telling him to take his pants off so she could tend to them. But Leizer wouldn't listen to her because that would have meant taking off his shoes, and since he was already late, he tried to dry the pants without taking them off, using the shop iron. But between the water and the hot iron it created such a burning steam that he screamed and in the end he had to take off his pants. He had burned his thigh so badly that it left a permanent scar. His mother treated it by spreading butter on the burn, the way everyone did at the time, because in those days you didn't go to the hospital for such a thing, or even the pharmacist. He was still in bed the next day when Yankel went to see him to find out why he hadn't come to the dance, and when they shared the stories of their evenings, nothing was ever the same.

"What I didn't know was that they were both in love with me. What's strange is that despite their friendship, or maybe to protect their friendship, they had never spoken about it together. Since I didn't know, I never had to hide anything. It was nice that way. And then this dance happened . . ."

"What if it had been Papa who for some reason hadn't come to the dance that evening? Do you think you would have married Leizer first?"

"Leizer . . . I don't know . . . I can't say. . . . No, I don't think so, because when your father asked me to marry him, right after we had kissed, it was so amazing, I don't know how to explain it. . . . You see, dancing in his arms was delightful, but dancing, kissing, and being asked to marry all in the same night, that was one of my greatest moments of happiness. Afterward, there were other great moments of happiness: your birth, Alex's birth. But that was the first. It was like a new world. It wasn't like we made plans for the future, it was better. It was already there, as if we were already married. I never had any regrets. But at the same time, who knows. . . . You know, I was thinking about all that earlier, in the film, when Jeanne Moreau arrived late for her appointment with Jim. It was something silly, like Leizer's burn. She goes to the hairdresser while Jim is waiting for her, and when she arrives at the café an hour late, Jim isn't there any more and she thinks he's the one who didn't show up. So the next day she leaves for Germany with Jules and marries him. And since war breaks out between France and Germany, they're separated for five years. You see, a stained pair of pants, a hairdresser appointment—sometimes little things like that change the course of an entire life."

My mother was just following the chronology of her story naturally, without seeking to give it any particular shape. As if having remained silent for so long had allowed her to preserve her memories intact. Her words, liberated by the film she had just seen, were nonetheless punctuated by silences, during which I tried to get my bearings. Things could so easily have been different—it wasn't hard to imagine that, but for an accident, I could have been Leizer's son.

"And Leizer? You said nothing was ever the same."

"Yes, he felt betrayed. By me, but especially by Yankel. He didn't want to see us as much. And gradually we realized that he was heartbroken. If it hadn't been for Leizer's heartbreak, our happiness would have been perfect. We didn't want to lose him and it was awful to feel that our love was destroying him. We would have liked to help him, but there was nothing either Yankel or I could do. We missed our friendship, and yet we were happy without him. We married in 1937. In November, shortly before Hanukah. It was a beautiful wedding. We sang, we danced, there was an orchestra and all our friends were there."

"Leizer was there too?"

"Yes, of course, he had to be there. He was even the one who made your father's wedding suit. A suit with a vest. It was his gift. For himself, he made a light-colored suit, a little too light for a wedding. He was also the one who seemed the most joyful, the happiest to be there. Unfortunately he drank too much. He had a bottle of vodka in his hand and was clinking glasses with everyone. We realized that his seeming joy was just an act, a way to hide his sadness. Then he got out of control. We couldn't stop him. He decided to teach us all a song in French. He wanted to teach all the guests. I don't know how he knew the song. You know the song 'Alouette, gentille alouette, alouette, je te plumerai.' It's a song you sang at summer camp. Before they met me, he and Yankel had planned to come to France one day, but I only learned that later. So at the wedding he sang, 'Je te plumerai le bec,' and while everyone else echoed, 'Je te plumerai le bec,' he drank a shot of vodka, and on and on. At the end, when everyone was singing in chorus, 'Et le bec, et les yeux, et la tête, et le cou, et les ailes,' Leizer looked at me and burst out crying. And almost at the same moment I saw a stain start to form on his pants. While the guests were singing, Leizer was crying and the stain on his pants was growing. Everyone chalked it up to drinking, and some even thought it was funny. It was awful. Maybe because of the way he was looking at me, I could see that his entire body was crying. And all I could do was watch."

My mother squeezed my arm a little tighter, and I thought for a moment her story was going to stop there—since leaving the movie theater, I had realized that a painful story is also made up of silence. I didn't dare ask any more questions. She continued her story after a few more steps, fearing, perhaps, that the story would get lost inside her. A story that kept the two men she had loved alive.

"Shortly after that your father and I decided to come live in France. I was sad for Leizer because it had been one of his plans, but I was afraid that if we stayed he would spoil our happiness.

We wrote to him from Paris several times, but he never answered our letters. The night before we left, we spent a long time together. We all cried, just as we had all laughed together before. And then came the war."

We had just passed the Rex movie house and the café where my mother, Leizer, Alex, and I would stop for ice cream or hot chocolate during our Sunday afternoon strolls.

"Do you remember the 'Boulevard Game'?" my mother asked, smiling at the mention of it.

Leizer had thought up this game. He would take us on Sundays to the odd side of the Boulevard Saint-Martin, and, starting from the Place de la République, pretending to be testing my progress in reading, he would teach himself Paris. We would walk side by side, he with his back to the shops, telling us the names of each one, while I would face the shops, eyes gazing upward—I must have been seven years old—approving or whispering the names that stumped him. That's what we did, Sunday after Sunday, until he learned the order of the names and signs by heart and with no hesitation. My mother, who followed us, pushing Alex in his carriage, laughed about it, but not without remarking to Leizer how childish it was to get such a kick out of knowing the names of the shops by heart, most of which he would never even enter. Leizer's only reaction, as if all his dreams of Paris were contained right there on that boulevard, would be to take Alex in his arms and sing with his Yiddish accent:

I love to wander the big boulevards
There are so many things, so many things,
So many things to see,

The cafés and their bars
And the terrace charms
Where the fancy ladies lounge.

We knew this route well. On the other side of the boulevard, there was always an orchestra on the terrace of the Café le Balthazar, opposite the variety and lingerie store. We would listen to two or three songs and go home.

With these old times reawakened—my mother had also looked over at the Balthazar, where the terrace at this time of year was covered—I felt I could ask her if she thought that my father would have been happy to know she'd married Leizer.

"Who knows. I often wondered that myself, and I could never find an answer. And now, where they both are . . . Yankel in ashes over the Polish sky, Leizer somewhere at the bottom of the ocean. . . . They probably won't meet up to talk," she continued with a grin. "The fact that you and Alex are here, alive, gives each of them an existence, since there is nowhere to go to pray for them, to watch over them. . . . There are the chairs where they sat, the bed where they slept, but Leizer never took Papa's place. They were each with me the same amount of time. Even though neither one is here, they're still sufficiently present so that no one else can come take their place."

Two men, one after the other, had disappeared from her life. Two men, one of them my father, about whom I could finally ask questions, because my mother had just broken a silence she had kept for so long.

"Do we know how Papa got caught?"

"No, we don't know exactly. I've told you the story of how we hid during the war. It was the shoe manufacturer that Papa worked for who told us the Jews would be rounded up the next day. We escaped the roundup by finding a place to hide in Gentilly, with someone Papa knew who was also working in leather. We quickly gathered a few things and stayed there, in Gentilly, sleeping four of us in one room. Bubbe was with us. After a few days, the person we were hiding with went to see what was going on in our neighborhood. We'd given him the keys, but he didn't go in because the doors were sealed. But we still had to get our things. Especially papers we might need, because we'd been in such a rush to leave we left a lot of things. I didn't want Papa to go back because everyone knew him in the neighborhood, and I didn't know who we could really trust. So he had the idea of entering by the rooftop, passing over the roof of the Winter Circus so as not to attract attention. He went several times to gather up what was there. He only took light things. Papers, a shoebox with all our photographs, some of your toys. He broke the seals, disgusted at the idea of having to break into his own home. And then one day he didn't come home. Was he turned in? Had someone seen that the seals were broken and been on the lookout for him? We never knew. The friend who was hiding us went back to see what was going on, but no one could tell him anything. Maybe he was stopped in the metro— they may have wanted to see what he had in his suitcase. I've imagined every possibility and to this day I don't know."

"Did you ask at the Winter Circus?"

"When? After the war? Two years later, who could I ask? In the beginning, I didn't ask anyone. Later, when I started to meet some deportees, I would show them his photo, but no one could tell me anything. I even asked Leizer, thinking they might have met at the camp, but I don't even know which camp Yankel was taken to. . . . I worried each time he would go home via the rooftops. I didn't want him to go back, but he insisted, he was sure nothing would happen to him. Leizer was the same way. I told him to go to New York by boat, that it was safer that way, but he wouldn't even discuss it. He thought he would get back more quickly this way. So he bought his plane ticket and he didn't even get to America where his sister was waiting for him."

We had arrived at the Winter Circus without even noticing. That's when my mother told me she didn't know where to mourn.

"There are memories," she continued, almost speaking to herself, "but you can't pray over a memory. Memories are made to be kept. There are photos . . . yes, there are photos, but in the photos they're alive. There are also cemeteries, but when I go to the one in Bagneux for Yom Kippur, I know that my loved ones aren't buried there. All there are are squirrels. So many squirrels in Bagneux. In the cemetery in Przytyk, there are also many squirrels. When I was little and saw them jumping from tomb to tomb, I couldn't help thinking they played a role in communicating between the dead and the living."

I had never felt so close to my mother as that night. Maybe it had been my all-too-brief love story, whose memories existed only inside me, that brought her own story to the surface, intact, with words she could finally tell me.

"I'm a little sad there isn't more of you in the film," she told me, "but I'm so glad to have seen it with you, and to have been able to talk about myself for the first time when I was about your age. Not only talk about myself, talk about myself to you. I think that's what was important . . . just by myself, I was afraid my loved ones would go away."

It had taken a film for me to finally hear this story—a story that is, in part, my own.

When we entered the gate to the Cité Crussol, I got goosebumps. Here was a woman, my mother, her arm in mine, telling me what she had never been able to tell me, never known how to tell me before. When we reached the back building, I looked up at the top story, where often at night a light in the kitchen window indicated that she was home.

When she cleans the windows, she sometimes stops, looks up at the rooftops and then down at the alley where the men she loved no longer pass. Usually it's in the morning, when the sun reaches inside our apartment, changing the color of the walls.

5

My mother was already at work and Alex at school when I woke up. On the table, a glass of orange juice covered by a little plate was waiting for me, along with a bowl for coffee and a fresh baguette. There was no note near the bowl, as there usually is when my mother needs me to do something for her. I knew that the milk and butter were in the fridge, and the coffee in the coffee pot, ready to be reheated.

As I drank my coffee, I tried to contemplate the effect the evening we had just spent together had had on my mother. I kicked myself for not having sensed her sorrow before.

I looked around me: there were no signs of the two men who had lived here, one after the other. Men who had loved my mother and whom my mother had loved. Only the photo of my father sitting on the sideboard, and next to the sideboard, like a piece of clothing no one wears, leaning against the wall, a chair that had become useless. The one in which my father and then Alex's father had sat, on which Alex would put his briefcase when he came home from school and on which my mother, a little later, would place her bag when she got home from work. That's when

I realized that the shoe box where I knew she kept the family photos was sitting on the corner of the table.

Unable to sleep, she had probably looked at some pictures and forgotten to put the box away.

So after placing my bowl in the sink, I removed the lid from the box—probably the same box my father had salvaged, passing over the rooftops, on which the word "photographs" was written in red pencil in my mother's precise handwriting. At the time I had no idea how far these photographs would take me. I wasn't expecting anything in particular. Not that I didn't value the photos, but those that had interested me until now were essentially related to the present. I looked at them a little distractedly. Piled one on top of the other, and mixed in with a few postcards that Alex and I had sent from the summer camp at Tarnos, were photos of when we were little, class photos, and others on heavy stock paper that showed people I didn't know and which I passed over. One of them, however, which was upside down in the pile, caught my attention because of a stamp that read: ART PHOTOGRAPHY, 32 RUE DE MÉNILMONTANT, PARIS, XXTH ARRONDISSEMENT, but with no mention of the date or the name of the photographer. It was a portrait in profile of my parents, the light filtering in from the side, the way they do it in photographic studios. As I continued to dig in the box, I found four other copies, all in postcard format. Why five copies? To send to the family in Poland? If that was the case, I figured that this photo must have dated from 1940, the year when correspondence with Poland became difficult. Hence the five copies that remained in the box.

My attention then turned to another photo: one of the shoe manufacturer where my father had worked as a top piece cutter.

You could see him in the picture, on the right side of the workshop, dressed in a white shirt with the sleeves rolled up. It was a large-format sepia photo glued to a gray piece of cardboard whose edges had been rubbed away. I must have already looked at this photo carefully, because it had a caption written in my handwriting in black pen: "This photo was taken at three fifteen." I was amused by this added information, written when I was a child—based on the writing I must have been eight—whereas in the photo, the wall clock is relatively hard to read. Then, among the photographs, I found a piece of paper connected to this photo: a work certificate on a piece of letterhead, furnished by my father's employer. His name was Leon Brandwain, 2 bis Rue Julien-Lacroix. The typewritten text said: "I the undersigned certify the employment of Mr. Appelbaum in my factory as a top piece cutter." It was dated June 13, 1941, signed by Brandwain, and stamped by the Belleville neighborhood police commissioner. This prompted me to pick up the photo and a loupe in order to see the so-called factory up close. There were eight workers, including one woman (would that be Mrs. Brandwain?) and an apprentice. But in the picture, they seemed to be playacting. The one who seemed to be the oldest—Mr. Brandwain perhaps—was proudly holding up one of his models. The use of the loupe allowed me to pay greater attention to certain details. Such as realizing that contrary to what I had written, this photo wasn't taken at three fifteen, but at a quarter to four.

Another photograph was taken by the photographer on the Rue de Ménilmontant. This time, I was the subject. The oval-shaped blur that surrounds my face, an artistic device common to studio photographers, makes it impossible to know what kind of clothes

I was wearing. All you can see is a wide round collar which covers my shoulders almost entirely. I must have been wearing a bib. As far as I can tell, I was about a year old. If this photograph was taken the same day as the one of my parents, which would make sense, it would have been about 1941. I find only one copy of this photograph in the box, which like the other is also in postcard format—on the back, on the right-hand side, there are even four lines for writing in the address. Were the others sent? If so, then until when was correspondence with Poland still possible? Another photograph is really the one that prompts this question for me. It is barely any larger than a passport photo. It shows a grandfather wearing a striped cloth cap with a prominent visor, the kind Russians and Poles generally wear. His face looks emaciated. Two deep folds begin at his nose and work their way down into his white mustache. His beard, which is also white, isn't shaped the way religious Jews usually wear their beards, but is shorter, a little squared off. He is also wearing a tie knotted around a thick cloth shirt, a cloth you can see isn't made for a tie. And most important, the yellow star which all Jews in occupied Europe were forced to wear is sewn on the right side of his chest. Maybe this is how you look at the world when you are looking at it for the last time. This man was my grandfather. My father's father. On the back of the photograph is a single notation, written in black pen: "13 × 18." A mere reference to an enlargement?

In order to recognize my father in the photo at the shoe workshop on the Rue Julien-Lacroix, I had to refer to the one that sits on the sideboard. In so doing, I was almost startled to notice one of the photos I had already taken out of the shoe box. A photo I'd glanced at quickly, but hadn't examined closely. My father and Leizer are sitting in the grass, leaning against a tree, shoulder to shoulder, and as if to better fill out the frame, they are posing with their legs stretched not in front of them but to the side. The many trees behind them lead me to believe they are in the woods near Przytyk. It must have been nice weather because they are both in shirtsleeves, but they've nonetheless kept their ties. Their pants are held up by thick suspenders. They almost look like twins. A jacket is hanging from a tree branch, at the foot of which sit two hats. A man's hat and a woman's hat. While the presence of my father and Leizer together in the picture caught my attention, it's the woman's hat that fascinated me. Because to my mind it couldn't have belonged to anyone else but my mother, and she is obviously the one taking the picture. Unlike in the image of my grandfather, my father and Leizer see the person they are looking at. They see who is photographing them, the woman they love. The look in their eyes, even more than the hat, reveals her presence. That's what this photograph is about: a love story.

"I lost my Jules and I lost my Jim," my mother had said, and I came to realize that these photographs in which her memories reside would give me answers if I asked them the right questions. Yet I wasn't asking them questions. I was merely looking at them, as attentively as possible. But maybe that too is a way of asking questions.

It was after looking at this photograph that something started taking shape, started seeping in. Tentatively at first, I developed something like a practice of research, inquiries, investigations, and patient digging in order to learn what came before.

This photograph was showing me a path to follow. It was like an invitation to rediscover what I had been missing until then. And I wondered, since it represented the image that my mother, my father, and Leizer had wanted to preserve of themselves, why it wasn't also placed on the sideboard, next to my father.

I poured a little more coffee, which I drank standing up, looking at the table with the scattered photos next to their box. At that moment it struck me that my mother had not simply forgotten to put the box away. She must have left it there, sitting on the table near the bowl, the orange juice, and the fresh baguette, hoping to continue the conversation we had begun only hours earlier.

And then came my parents' wedding photo. Placed first, at the bottom of the box—thus the last for me—it was like the missing piece of a puzzle. There it was, in this shoe box, simply waiting for me to pick it up. For me to notice it. My loupe in hand, I examined it as if it would put my life in order.

Strangely, unless there are others elsewhere, it wasn't the usual type of wedding photo, in which the bride and groom are standing alone, surrounded by flowers.

In this photo, my father and mother are sitting at the end of a table. As if they are thinking of the days to follow, something both sweet and serious seems to be clouding their faces. Bubbe is sitting next to my mother, wearing a dress familiar to me. Next to my father is his own father, whom I now recognize, even though his beard isn't yet white, and, seated next to him, an old woman who must be my paternal grandmother. The others, about twenty of them, are standing in a semicircle around the newlyweds. Here too, no doubt at the request of the photographer, they are looking at him and smiling, something some of them must have done spontaneously. Everybody but Leizer. Sitting to the extreme left of the photo, in the first row, disregarding the photographer's instructions, his face is turned toward my father and mother.

I now know, even though his face is turned, that he is looking at them with resentment, a hurt from which he couldn't heal. In contrast to my father's dark suit, its breast pocket amply decorated with a white handkerchief, Leizer is wearing a light-colored suit.

I also know that this photograph was taken before his despair led him to the "Alouette, gentille alouette" episode.

As I lingered over the serene smiles of my parents, as if reminding myself of a time before my birth, I realized I was neglecting to think about Leizer. He had come back from hell long enough to marry the woman he loved and to have a child with her. After which, he had plunged into the ocean. Before this, I never asked any questions, because he had always seemed to me to know everything. This man, the father of my little brother, was always there, a number tattooed on his arm, spending his time trying to make up for lost time. As with the "Boulevard Game," he had wanted to see, to possess almost, all the places that over the years he had imagined through books and had never stopped dreaming of.

I remember that one Sunday we all took the train to the countryside. We ate on the grass and played ball. But Leizer wanted first and foremost to find a place that had been described in a French book he had read in Yiddish before the war. Later, I learned he had been looking for Cosette's house in Montfermeil, and that he'd been horribly disappointed to learn that it was merely the fruit of Victor Hugo's imagination.

Alouette, gentille alouette,
Alouette je te plumerai.

I'm not sure what I was expecting of these images, the observation and dogged exploration of which brought me closer and closer to the dead. Did they contain an element of something I didn't know I needed? But something struck me. A photograph was missing: one in which we were all together, me seated on my mother's knees, her arms encircling me in sweetness and warmth. Sitting next to her would be the reassuring presence of my father, whose left hand, with his wedding ring, would be resting on her right. And we would all be looking at the photographer.

It was close to noon when I finished carefully replacing the photos in their box and went out onto the stairwell. I unhooked the ladder from the wall that we used to climb to the roof. Through the open dormer window, I spent a long time looking at the imposing mass of the Winter Circus. Around me, the snow fallen overnight covered the zinc roofs.

6

When my mother had finished reading *Jules and Jim*, she asked me if I knew when and how Jules had died.

"No, why?"

"Because Jules was Jewish."

"Really? How do you know that?"

"It's written in the book. Look, page 31: ' . . . one morning, Hermann, a friend of mine, grabbed my napkin from me, threw it on the ground, and punched me in the nose saying: You're a dirty Jew. I bled without understanding, but that night my mother explained it to me.' We know that Jim is Henri Pierre Roché, the book's author, but I'd love to know what Jules's real name was."

So I began reading *Jules and Jim*, and from the first page, I found François Truffaut's film almost to the letter. In the first pages, I also found a description of the moment when Jules sketches a woman's face on a restaurant table. The face of a woman he would have loved if it hadn't been for Lucie, who, Jules explains, was a girl from his home town whose hand he had asked for in marriage but who had turned him down. Strangely, despite being so present in the book, in which entire chapters are devoted to her—"Jules and Lucie," "Lucie and Jim," "Lucie in Paris," "The Travels of Lucie"—this Lucie was absent from the film. Just as others, who appear later on in the book, were gone: Gertrude, Lina, Magda, and Odile.

When Henri Pierre Roché wrote, speaking of Lucie, "She said no . . . but so gently that I'm still hoping," Laura's face almost naturally superimposed itself on each sentence. "She gave Jim her long trembling hands." "She gave him, through her hair, contact with her lips." And like Jim, because of the "perfect little times they had had together," I got choked up when they separated.

With the book in my pocket, I decided to head to Chez Victor to continue reading. I hadn't been to this bistro on the Impasse Compans in over eight months—since the day of that parting kiss with Laura. There was hardly anyone there now, in the early afternoon. "My" place was free, so I sat down. After ordering a hot chocolate from Mr. Victor, I reminded him who I was.

"With Jeanne Moreau? Of course I remember. I even saw in the newspaper that the film was out in theaters.

"Yes, two weeks ago."

"And? Do you see my bistro?"

"Yes, yes. Several times even."

"Wonderful. Do you know when it will be on TV?"

"No, I don't. But since it just came out, I doubt it will be anytime soon."

"Okay, well, I'll wait. Because I hardly ever leave my bistro. Just to get the bread and croissants for the bar before I open. And on Sundays I go to the Place des Fêtes for shopping. The rest I get delivered. Alright, I'll go make your hot chocolate."

On rereading the pages that talk about Lucie here, at Chez Victor, I had the impression I could feel Laura close to me, even though it had been so long since I'd seen her; I didn't even want to turn the pages so that I could stay with Lucie, who brought me close to Laura. Interestingly, in the chapters concerning Lucie, here and there a phrase appeared, a thought it seemed to me I'd already heard: "Don't cause suffering, Jim . . ." And further on: "Jim, love her, marry her, and let me see her. What I mean is: if you love her, don't think of me as an obstacle." And then this, which I was sure I'd heard in the film: "All the yearning that travels from heart to heart, my God, my God! What suffering it brings."

I closed the book, and with a different sort of curiosity, I returned that very night to the Cinema le Vendôme to see *Jules and Jim* again. I had been right: all these phrases in the book were in the film, but attributed to Catherine. And the role of Catherine, which I loved, really belonged to Lucie, who wasn't in the film. Truffaut had given Catherine Lucie's role.

On the radio I heard a writer—I don't know who it was because I heard the program in passing—say that his pleasure in reading was often linked to a place. He explained that he read Giono on the banks of the Durance River, Maupassant in Normandy, Henri Calet on the number 96 bus. It was this last example— since the 96 passes in front of my house on its way to Lilas, via the Rue de Ménilmontant—that inspired me to read *Jules and Jim* at Chez Victor, feeling that it was obviously the best place.

When Mr. Victor saw me again, he extended his hand over the bar. The zinc, as he called it.

"Want your hot chocolate on the zinc?"

He thought drinking at the bar was better for conversation.

Behind the bar, tacked underneath the calendar, was a photograph taken in the bistro. In the foreground was the "Godin" stovepipe which crossed through the room and which you could still hear snoring. Next to it was a man in a cap, standing like a regular at the bar, cigarette in hand, staring into space, seemingly oblivious to the photographer. As was a lady behind the bar, her left hand holding up her chin. Who was she? Mrs. Victor? I didn't ask.

But Mr. Victor followed my gaze, and told me, "That's from '55. A photographer who was taking pictures in the neighborhood gave it to me. Because my bistro is historical. Look, I'll show you something."

And inviting me to come around behind the counter, he showed me a knob on the floor that lifted a kind of trap door.

"Does the young man know where that leads?" asked Monsieur Victor, in a more confidential tone.

"The basement, I imagine?"

"That's right. That's where I keep my wine. But not just the basement. It's an escape route. Well, it was an escape route," he continued, in answer to my inquisitive silence. "It leads to the Rue de Belleville, number 213, right at the corner of the Place des Fêtes. The gentleman can go, see, it leads to the second courtyard. There's a manhole. The 'lantern manhole' they call it. That's where it leads."

"Can you still get there through here?"

"No, not anymore. It's been walled off. But in the days of Bonnot, you could."

"Bonnot? The Bonnot gang?"

"Exactly! Bonnot from the Bonnot gang. But don't get me wrong, I didn't know him, because at the time I couldn't even reach the counter. It's the guy who sold me the place who told me. It turns out Bonnot came here often. But you know how there's always some goody-two-shoes who tells the cops, and since this was a dead end, they were sure to nab him. But by the time they got to the gate, Bonnot was already in the basement heading toward the lantern manhole or other manholes—the ones on the Rue des Cascades or the Rue de la Mare, because it seems they all connected. In the end, Bonnot ended up getting caught, but much later and not here. In Choisy-le-Roi. Hey, if you want to know more, there's a customer who comes here a lot and who knows all the stories about Belleville, the Commune, everything. He's an old guy whose hair is white like a snowy mountain. It's good to meet him because he knew everyone. Except that there's one thing he always regretted: he wishes he'd had Louise Michel, the famous revolutionary who was active during the Paris Commune, as a teacher. He could have. He was fifteen when she died. What I mean is that you learn as much listening to him as you do from reading books. This is about when he comes in," continued Mr. Victor, looking at an alarm clock sitting where he kept the glasses, "he brings me my *France-Soir*, he reads it, puts it on the zinc, and then leaves. Sometimes we play a little game of dice."

Some men from Piedmont, probably the ones I'd seen the last time, whom the dry cold air must have chased from the bocce court, went to sit in the second room.

"Gotta go for a second," said Mr. Victor, arranging glasses and a still-corked bottle of wine on a tray. "It's a Barbera," he said, pointing at the label, "a red I bring in special from Italy for them. They're former masons. It's all they drink. Well, sometimes in summer they drink a beer when it's hot, but otherwise, ten months of the year, it's this. I've tasted it: it's not to my taste but it's drinkable. It's like everything, a question of habit. Hey, you like hot chocolate, they like Italian wine."

"And they all live in the neighborhood?"

"Of course. A bistro's not a place you drive to." And off Mr. Victor went to serve them.

I finished my hot chocolate, but stayed at the bar. Because of the conversation.

"If you stay a minute," Mr. Victor told me, returning with his empty tray, "you'll hear them sing. You wouldn't believe it. They came to France before the war, when they were young, since we needed masons. They wanted to start a new life, leave the poverty in Italy behind, but their hearts never left. So they drink their local wine and they sing in Italian. But only old tunes, because you don't find that melancholy in the new ones. They even sing 'Le Chaland qui passe' in Italian."

And as if they had overheard Monsieur Victor, the Piedmontese, building up steam before starting their repertoire, belted out "Mamma" with just the right emotion.

"Listen, they always start there: 'Mamma, son tanto felice.' Because they can't get over having left their mamas."

Afterward, when they sang "E tutti va in Francia / in Francia per lavorare," the words of which were easy to understand, it seemed to me, by association, that I could even hear my mother singing "Belz, mein shtetele Belz," a Yiddish song about the regret of leaving the little shtetl in Poland too soon. One of those songs that are all about nostalgia.

And then there was "Bella ciao," which I sang along with them, and which I was proud to show Monsieur Victor that I knew.

O partigiano, portami via
O bella ciao, bella ciao, bella ciao, ciao ciao
O partigiano, portami via
Che mi sento di morir

"You know that one? How do you know it?"

"I learned it in summer camp."

"Was it an Italian summer camp?"

"No, no. It wasn't Italian. But that's the song of the Italian partisans. And since we had a choir at camp, they taught us partisan songs from several countries." In a state of amazement, Mr. Victor left to bring another bottle to the second room.

On the counter sat a copy of *France-Soir* from the day before. For several weeks now, the newspapers had been reporting on attacks committed by the Organization of the Secret Army, or OAS, in and around Paris. This time, according to the headline, the bomb that exploded seriously wounded a little girl named Delphine Renard, four and a half years old, who was playing with her doll. She may end up blind. The bomb was targeting the minister of cultural affairs, André Malraux.

I put off reading *Jules and Jim* and decided to go home.

That's when the door opened, and a white-haired man entered dressed in a thick corduroy vest, similar in every way to the one

Robert was wearing the day of the shoot. Closing the door behind him, he went to sit in the back of the room and removed a soft cap, which he rolled up and placed in his pocket. He moved slowly, almost methodically, unbuttoning each button of his vest and unfolding his newspaper, which he laid out before him.

I promised myself I'd be back.

7

Eight dead. The papers say the deaths were due to cranial trauma and suffocation at the end of an anti-OAS demonstration that took place February 8. Eight dead. That's the count of the police clampdown. Eight dead, including Daniel Ferry, fifteen. Alex's age. Eight dead, including Fanny Dewerpe, thirty years old, found lifeless at the Boulets-Montreuil metro. Fanny had been a counselor at the Tarnos summer camp. She had already lost her husband in 1952, during a demonstration against the visit to France of General Ridgway. She leaves behind a young son, Alain, ten years old. I learned from the newspaper that she lived at 97 Rue Oberkampf. Right near me.

The funeral is scheduled for Tuesday, February 13. The procession will leave at 10 AM from the stock exchange, where the bodies of the eight victims will be available for viewing. It will pass by the Place de la République, the Avenue de la République, up the Boulevard de Ménilmontant all the way to the main entrance of the Père-Lachaise cemetery.

There will be no banners, no placards, no flags, no slogans.

"Dress warm, it's raining and cold," said my mother, when at 8:30 AM the electricity suddenly went out. A work stoppage to honor the victims.

"Watch out for Alex," she added as we were heading out the door. I reassured her with a smile. We said nothing more to one another, but in our eyes you could read the same story. The story of the demonstration in Przytyk that had followed the pogrom, during which several people had also died, and during which she met my father and Alex's father.

My efforts to watch over Alex were short-lived. The immense crowd that continued well beyond the Boulevard des Filles-du-Calvaire separated us just past the Winter Circus.

On the Avenue de la République, where it crosses the Rue Oberkampf, as I was looking for the building where Fanny had lived, on the odd side of the street, I ran into Robert. The fact that Robert was at this procession wasn't surprising, but it was surprising that I would run into him in the midst of this enormous crowd, this mass of men and women wishing to follow the funeral procession of these lives cut short by the Paris police.

Before we got separated, just before reaching the Père-Lachaise cemetery, Robert talked about Fanny.

"I'm thinking about her child's suffering. What will they tell him? Will they talk to him about justice? Vengeance? Will they tell him about his parents' heroism, their courage, their struggle? Of course, I know we need to keep that image in mind, but first and foremost is his suffering. I was trying to imagine it, thinking back to those times in the summer camp, our poetry nights. Do you remember?"

It was not one comrade
But millions and millions
To take revenge, he knew,
And the day broke over him.

"That's it: 'And the day broke over him.' It was in 1943, I think, that Paul Eluard wrote that poem for a resistance fighter. Would he be writing it again today, if he were still alive? I'm not sure. I'm glad we had our poetry nights. We were right to put them on. At the time of the Liberation, it helped to dry the tears, but it didn't prevent our shedding other tears. When I was a tailor, I had a client who would often say to me, 'Tears are the only commodity that is never exhausted.' I didn't know at the time how true that was. A little while ago I ran into Janine, whom I also hadn't seen in a long time. She was at the demonstration Thursday night, near metro Charonne, where most of the deaths occurred. And she told me that it wasn't until she got home and watched it on television that she learned what had happened, and she suddenly realized—she had left her baby with a babysitter—that she could have left her own child an orphan, just as she had been, since her parents had been deported and she grew up in an orphanage. She was terrified at the thought that it could have started all over again with her own son, and she wouldn't have been able to give him what she had always dreamed of giving him, and which she herself had never received. She told me she only came today because of Fanny—and she could barely hold back her tears—but that she wouldn't demonstrate any more, she was too afraid."

In walking with Robert, I kept thinking that I had been

fourteen when he was twenty-two, and what struck me as I listened to him was not his anger but his despair, even though that's not how I remembered him.

We spoke about our plans. I still didn't know what I was doing. He told me that he had been thinking seriously about getting into television, because he was increasingly drawn to the idea of making documentaries, and that was where there was the most opportunity to do so. What had finally convinced him was that he had just learned that an adaption of the book *The Gates of the Louvre* was being made into a movie.

"What worries me is the way this project was presented," explained Robert. "They said it was 'about the roundup of Jews that ended in ten thousand victims from the Temple and Marais neighborhoods.' That's it: just the Temple and Marais neighborhoods! And not other neighborhoods? So to escape the roundup, all you had to do was change neighborhoods? To pass the 'gates of the Louvre' and stay on the left bank? So then why were Beck, Bzegowski, Brechner, Moskowitz, and all my friends from the Butte-aux-Cailles rounded up? What kind of history lesson is this? I don't know how the film will turn out, maybe people will be moved, but I know we shouldn't be telling fictional stories. History has to be told by its victims, by those who lived it."

We lost one another shortly after that. Just when a gust of rain and hail pounded the procession. But I did have time to ask him if he knew what had become of the Jules in *Jules and Jim*. He didn't know. He only knew that his real name was Franz Hessel.

It was near the Communards' Wall that I left the procession. That was where, among the big old chestnut trees with their leafless branches and the grave of Jean-Baptiste Clément, I saw the

man with the white hair who brought Monsieur Victor his newspaper every day, wearing a felt hat with its brim lowered. An outfit
straight out of the Paris Commune, the same Gallic mustache, the
same scarf, the same hat as Jean-Baptiste Clément, who wrote "Le
Temps des Cerises." As he watched the crowd pass, close to those
being laid to rest, he seemed a figure out of the past, as if the dead
of February 8 were a rebirth of the Commune.

That was how I just naturally ended up at the café in the Impasse Compans the very next day.

Seated at the same table as the previous day, the white-haired
man was reading a newspaper article aloud.

Chez Victor was no ordinary café. You could tell by looking at
the faces as they listened to his reading. Though some were holding glasses absentmindedly in their hands, they hadn't come there
out of thirst. They were listening with special attention, as if the
words contained something they'd lost:

" 'The crowd's first rows reached Père-Lachaise before the
back of the line could even start walking. Paris hasn't seen such
a funerary procession for years. How many were they, these men
and women clustered together, slowly climbing the Avenue de la
République behind the bodies of the eight protesters killed on
February 8? And the flowers! A sea of flowers. From the heights
of Ménilmontant, these flowers were like a walking garden, slowly
inundating the Avenue de la République. One of the most beautiful and most unforgettable images Paris has ever offered to
those who love her people. Along with the flowers, what was most
striking was the silence. The crowd didn't utter a sound, not a
word. You could just barely hear the slow shuffling of this fan-
tastic column on the wet ground, accompanying the dead to the

heights of the city in the glacial wind, the gusts of rain and hail.
You didn't see a policeman or security agent all morning. And
never was a cortege more orderly, more disciplined, more reveren-
tial. Among the procession were miners with their hard hats and
lamps. Deportees wore their striped pajamas from twenty years
ago. The fabric washed out, faded, gray as an old flag. After the
flowers, others were carrying photos of the victims. In the back,
alone, was the photo of little Daniel Ferry. The face of a child.
He is smiling, a smile that brings tears to all who see him. The
photo was followed immediately by the child's hearse, covered in
white.' "

Standing in the doorway, I watched these men and women, whose
silence seemed an extension of the silence mentioned in the article.

What they were hearing was not just an account of what had
happened the day before. A piece of them was coming back to life,
revived by the movement of the words.

Near me, a twelve-year-old boy was sitting in front of a glass of
grenadine he hadn't touched. A woman sitting nearby moved her
chair closer to his and put her arms around him.

No one moved when the man with the white hair, after finishing the article, headed for the bar. You could see his lips trembling. He announced the reading of an excerpt from Victor
Hugo's "L'Enterrement."

The drum beats in the fields, and the flag bows.
From the Bastille to the foot of the mournful hill
Where centuries past near the century living
Sleep beneath the cypress trees undisturbed by the wind,

The people are armed; the people are sad; they think
and their great ranks silently form a guard.
The son dead and the father yearning at the grave
Pass, yesterday one still brave, hale and hearty,
The other old, hiding the tears on his face;
And each legion salutes them in passing.

His lips had not stopped trembling but his voice carried throughout the room. The fighter of the Paris Commune was somehow channeled through this man today, and the verses were spoken as if transporting the listeners to a native land. Hugo's words struck a chord, and those present, working-class people who were proud of their status, relished hearing themselves reflected in them.

Cast back to her youth and no doubt to her life struggles by this emotional moment, a woman with a thick woolen shawl over her shoulders, held in place by a fat diaper pin, spontaneously began to sing "Le Temps des Cerises," without budging from her spot:

When we will sing the time of the cherries
And the cheerful nightingale, and mocking blackbird
Will be all in celebration!

These men and women among whom I hadn't dared sit, whose memories I felt separated them from me, were showing me images of their past from which they knew they would never heal. They didn't have to recall this "Time of the Cherries," which the woman's voice had evoked—this song was a faithful companion and had never left them. It took over the room.

I who fear not hard losses
I will not live without suffering one day.

I was reminded of *Casque d'Or*, which I had seen again after
what Robert had told me about it. This was the tune to which
Simone Signoret and Serge Reggiani waltzed, as in the first days
of their romance.

Evening was approaching when I left Monsieur Victor's bistro.
A gas lamp—a real one—lit the bocce court, revealing details
of the stage on its little legs. Far from the crowds, this place had
been part everyday café, part Saturday night dance hall, the com-
pensation for a hard week's work. What had changed that no one
danced there anymore?

I was thinking about Laura, who inevitably came to mind,
when I heard "It's a real moment in history."

It was the lady, accompanied by the boy with the grenadine,
who was offering this take on events as she walked past me. In
suggesting that this moment would be remembered, what was she
alluding to? The place itself, which I felt I was discovering for the
first time today? What we had just witnessed? I responded with a
slight smile and watched her leave, holding her son's hand. She had
no idea how much her simple words had moved me.

This place and this moment would become inseparable.

As if this day were guiding me, I made my way effortlessly to
the Rue Piat, where I had run into Robert photographing the Villa
Ottoz one year earlier. And this recent past seemed so long ago.

Lingering a moment near the metal ramp where we had stood
silently gazing at Paris, I took in the illuminated facades, Nadine's
bistro next to the Villa Faucheur, the Villa Castel a bit further

along, which was visible in Truffaut's film, the stairs of the Rue Vilin, the washed-out, burgundy facade of the Repos de la Montagne, and the ocher bakery to which the ramp was attached. I had never taken Robert's advice and returned on an early April morning, but I will go there right now for a chocolate croissant.

I was beginning to realize that the places I had passed, looking at them without taking the trouble to really see them, were just like the photographs my father had saved; they were responding to a need. Something about my surroundings was becoming clear, falling into place. These photographs, these places were grabbing hold of me: not yet memories, they somehow constituted my essence, and without knowing it I would become nostalgic for them. Thus, descending the Rue Vilin, whose irregular paving stones forced me onto the sidewalk, I discovered the shutters of Madame Rayda's.

It was just past the wood and coal dealer at the base of the stairs, on the ground floor of a yellow house. The shutters were large and wide open, and posted on the right was a carefully written sign which until then had never caught my attention.

MADAME RAYDA

CHALDEAN TAROT READER

ASTROLOGY——GRAPHOLOGY——MEDIUM

PALM READING——INK BLOTS

CLAIRVOYANCE VIA PHOTO AND CORRESPONDENCE

RETURN OF AFFECTION

OPEN EVERY DAY

FROM 2 PM TO 7 PM

RUE VILIN 47

PARIS 20TH

METRO COURONNES

And above it all, a drawing of a wide-open hand, along with three playing cards, one of which was an ace of spades. But strangely, there was nothing about the future.

8

A few weeks later, on a Saturday afternoon, I went to the flea market at Saint-Ouen. More in the mood to seek than to find, I was enjoying meandering these sidewalks where I can never manage to see everything, where everything is up for grabs, where all these tangled memories intersperse, and even decompose sometimes. I liked that this place was faithful to its own disorder.

I always went first to the Chope des Puces, a bistro on the Rue des Rosiers, located just after the Biron market, to listen to a trio of gypsy guitarists. They weren't always the same three who played at the Chope, but you knew that on Saturday and Sunday afternoons, you could hear that particular jazz, invented by Django Reinhardt. They even claimed he had played there. As evidence, on the back wall, enclosed in a glass case, sat a guitar with a little sign indicating it had belonged to him. They claimed as well that the musicians who still played there were members of his family. Cousins. Which must have been partly true because I had had occasion to hear his son, Babik, there, playing in an equally ample style with the same sense of swing, yet without imitating his father.

That day there was only one guitarist. An accordion replaced the two others. As a result, it was more of a "dance jazz" repertory. They played the inevitable and ever-popular "Nuages" and "Minor Swing," of course, but also popular tunes by Gus Viseuer or Jo Privat such as "Manouche Party."

An hour later, I went to see Max, a friend from the summer camp who ran a booth with his father just opposite the Paul-Bert market. Since the father never had anything I needed, he had stopped trying to sell me anything. So we chatted a moment, sitting on some old armchairs awaiting their purchaser. But Max wasn't there. So I said good-bye to his father, whose photo in boxing gear presided over a dresser from the 1930s, and I continued along the Rue Jules-Vallès. You have to leave yourself time to wend your way down this street. And you have to bend over a lot. Because the finds of the week are displayed on the ground here, on pieces of old rugs. A child's toy, a rusty razor, a hotel ashtray, a pan for grilling chestnuts, an amputated doll, and other objects whose origins were difficult to determine. And in the midst of all this, unrelated to anything else, an allegedly rare book. An idler, with no particular plan to purchase anything but propelled by the desire for acquisition, might ask how much they want for a particular book.

In a more serious corner, resting on nearly three meters of boards propped on trellises, was an impressive collection of images lying in a heap, surrounded by a crowd immersing itself in these alleged treasures—real buyers this time, seeking to leave no image unturned, determined to save what to their minds deserved to be saved. Family photographs, the oldest ones printed on paper or cardboard, photographs of movie stars, generally in vertical format, with the name printed on the bottom—Edwige Feuillère, Danielle Darrieux—and in one carefully classified box, a group of postcards stamped with the figure of a sower. Ten cents for the red ones, five cents for the green. "It depends on the number of words," explained the merchant. "Kisses from Nice, that's five cents, ten cents if there's something more written about the sender's life. The signature doesn't count as a word." The card I had in my hands, written with a feather pen dipped in purple ink, was addressed to a Monsieur Marouly, Hôtel des Lilas, 35, Avenue Victoria, Vichy, Allier. My compunctions at that instant in prying into another person's memories—even though the postcard was mailed in 1916—were swept away by the image titled "Paris (XIth arrondissement)— Théâtre concert du Bataclan, Boulevard Voltaire." It read:

My Dear Uncle,

I received your postcard Tuesday morning. You were the first to welcome me to Paris, and I thank you. Your card is very pretty but the portrait of my future father-in-law isn't promising. If the son is cut from the same cloth I'd prefer he remain in Vichy. I don't want such an ugly husband and I'm sure you wouldn't want a monster for a nephew either. Father, Mother, and Grandfather send their best wishes. As for me, I send you a big kiss.

Your niece who loves you,
Laurence

More than the evocative correspondence which often overflowed onto the picture side of the postcard, it was the images of Paris from before World War I that interested me.

I found some postcards from my neighborhood which I put carefully aside: the Rue Oberkampf seen from the Rue Amelot, the school on the Rue Saint-Sebastien which Alex and I had attended, a view of the Rue d'Angoulême which became the Rue Jean-Pierre-Timbaud, the entrance to the metro at La République. Then, from the depths of the assorted images sprang an entire series of film photographs—almost a collection—into which several hands had begun digging feverishly.

The traces of thumbtacks visible in the four corners of the photographs, indicating that they had been tacked up in front of movie theaters, reminded me of the scene in *The 400 Blows* when Jean-Pierre Léaud steals a photo from a Bergman film.

Out of these fragments of film offerings, thinking of Alex, I had just managed to extract two photographs of the Marx Brothers—Harpo, Chico, and Groucho in *At the Circus*, and Harpo in *A Night at the Opera*—when a woman's hand appeared bearing another photo of Harpo decked out in a visor and typing on a typewriter, and I heard: "This one might also interest you." I thanked the woman with a smile and was already imagining how happy it would make Alex, whose affection for Harpo approached veneration.

I had brought Alex to see a film by the Marx Brothers as soon as I considered him capable of reading subtitles. He must have been seven or eight. It was *The Big Store*, and he had been so blown away to see three guys on the screen doing exactly what he would have liked to do in life that he had made Harpo his spiritual guide. But this was something I only realized gradually.

That night, at the dinner table, he had said that in addition to roller skates for his upcoming birthday, he would also like a raincoat like the one Harpo wore, with deep pockets. And he had added: "When I grow up, I want to be a silent actor." Bubbe was the first to comment:

"A silent actor? That's a new one. Is that all you could come up with? Just a silent actor? If you started by being mute in life, wouldn't that be smarter? You think you can become mute just like that? Just by going to the movies?"

Bubbe's reaction had at least two explanations.

Since she was close to fifty when she arrived in France, just before the war, she had decided that it was too late to learn a new language, and she always spoke to us in Yiddish. Which meant that Alex and I understood Yiddish without speaking it, and that for Bubbe it was exactly the opposite: she ended up understanding our French responses without knowing how to speak French. The same for reading. She could only understand what she read in the newspaper if she read it out loud. Which was why, when she took Alex to the movies one day to see a western at my mother's request and it turned out that the film had subtitles, she couldn't help but read the subtitles out loud, as she did with the newspaper. Thus she treated the others in the audience to a recitation of John Wayne's lines, spoken with a Yiddish accent. Which explains the state of fury and embarrassment Alex was in when he returned home, swearing that it was the last time he would set foot in a movie theater with Bubbe.

Under the German occupation, it was decided Bubbe should be mute. Since the words coming out of her mouth were all stamped with a yellow star, she couldn't say a thing once she stepped outside. Which wasn't without its difficulties, as I later learned. She often took me to the Montsouris Park, near Gentilly where we were in hiding, and since she couldn't call out to me, she was obliged to run after me as soon as I threatened to wander off. There are no official statistics on the increase in the dumb among the population of recent Jewish immigrants from Eastern Europe who, after the Liberation—assuming they had survived—miraculously recovered their ability to speak. It's too bad, for I learned much later that many were afflicted with this disability. My mother told me that, since I insisted on calling my grandmother "Bubbe"—I was barely two years old—she was quickly spotted by another grandmother who used the same ruse.

While at the beginning the two of them were happy to merely greet one another with a nod of the head, they soon invented an entire series of gestures that allowed them to broaden their conversation. I often wondered, if chance had caused them to cross paths with a real deaf and dumb individual, what that person would have made of this invented sign language.

Because she thought she had played the role of a mute to perfection, my grandmother expressed the greatest reservations regarding Alex's acting ambitions.

The other reason, one which made for difficult relations between Bubbe and Alex, and which so upset Mother, was more painful.

For Bubbe, I naturally possessed every virtue because, in her mind, she was the one who had brought me up from an early age. Thus, despite the absence of a father in the house, she felt that the three of us—she, my mother, and I—had been just fine in our apartment in the Cité Crussol.

The real problem for Bubbe was the reappearance of Leizer. In her mind, Leizer was still the one who had sullied her daughter's wedding in front of all the guests, and who now was filling the empty slot. He was an intruder, a usurper, a power seeker.

But Leizer was none of those things. Alone after the war, he had found not just the woman he had never stopped loving, but a family, and for this he thanked his lucky stars.

It was mainly the arrival of Alex, however, that Bubbe viewed as an imminent threat. Already, when Leizer came to live in the house, the folding cot I slept on, which we unfolded at night and folded up again in the morning, had to be moved into the little room that served as my grandmother's bedroom. Which forced her—though she never complained—to undress in the dark. My mother knew what Alex's birth implied and for her it was an increasingly absorbing problem. Our apartment was getting too small, we had to find a room nearby for Bubbe to sleep in. And what was then just the end of her peaceful existence turned into a real source of anxiety.

After the moving plans were announced, the conversation my mother had dreaded took place.

"You had me come all the way from Poland and now you're kicking me out? I left everything for you: my friends, my house, your poor father's grave. If I had stayed there, at least I could have gone to his grave to speak with him. Now who goes to his grave to speak to him? The Poles? Even when he was alive they didn't speak to him."

"But Mother, how can you talk about Poland? There are no more Jews in Poland! You think there are still Jews there who remember you? You think there's a single Jew left in Przytyk to ask another Jew: Have you heard any news about Mrs. Horowitz? The Jews all died in the camps! They all went up in smoke. Even the graves in the Jewish cemeteries were ransacked!"

"And I suppose France is any better? Yankel wanted to see France and what did he see of France? He didn't have a chance to see anything. Just enough time to make a baby, may God bless him, and then he also went up in smoke. He called himself Jacques and a lot of good it did him. Was it worth leaving everything behind to go to a country where you don't know anyone?"

"It's true that Yankel is gone, but at least you're here, you're alive, you have a daughter, you have a grandson, and soon you'll have another one. And no one is kicking you out. Everything will be exactly as it is now, you'll always eat lunch and dinner with us. It's just for sleeping. And it will be better for you. I already asked the concierge to find something nearby. That way, even Bernard can come see you without leaving the Cité."

"So that's it, it's all set? The baby isn't even here and already I have to move?"

It was into this climate of tension that Mother came home from the Rothschild Hospital with Alex in her arms. Even though the concierge (after receiving a gratuity) had already found a little studio with a kitchen in a neighboring building, my mother had asked Bubbe to be there when she got home. That turned out to be a smart move. Shortly thereafter, against all expectations, my grandmother decided on her own to move to her studio. "Since I can't sleep at night anyway, I may as well be in my own place." She had said "my own place," so it was all for the best. In the end, even after Leizer perished in the airplane accident that took the lives of forty-eight people, she continued to sleep in her studio. Nevertheless, her relationship with Alex remained complicated.

When Alex was of the age that we now call "the sausage poop stage," if he happened to be home with a few friends and one of them said "poop," another said "peeny," and a third said "fart," they all doubled over laughing. By the time they got to "butt," they were rolling on the rug holding their tummies. And with "big boobies," they were close to convulsions. And on and on until they had exhausted their knowledge.

Shortly after he grew out of this phase, Alex asked me if I too had laughed at these types of jokes when I was little.

"Of course, like all kids do."

"And did Mother say anything to you?"

"No, I don't remember her saying anything. She must have figured it would pass, just as it passed with you."

"And Bubbe didn't say anything to you either?"

"Bubbe didn't either."

"She told me it was dirty. What kinds of things did you say?"

"What did I used to say? . . . I don't remember anymore what we used to say."

"Yes, you do, what did you say? You don't remember?"

"No, I don't remember. Oh yeah, do you want to trade?"

"What?"

"My butt for a lemonade?"

Alex just couldn't seem to wait to meet up with one of his friends to try out this rhyming joke. And the only person available at the time was Bubbe, darning socks in the dining room. It wasn't the best choice.

"Bubbe," I heard him say, "do you want to trade?"

"What?"

"Bernard's butt for a lemonade?"

The sound of a slap, and then Alex was back, tears streaming down his cheeks.

Several years passed before I understood why Alex had been so sad. This business of "Bernard's butt for a lemonade," which at the time had amused me, now devastated me. It wasn't Bubbe's slap that had brought Alex to tears, but the fact that he didn't understand why she had slapped him. What had he done? He had merely repeated what I had told him. And for that he was slapped?

It was during this period, before I understood, that I abusively and stupidly played on Alex's innocence. He had asked me why he always had the impression that my father, in the photo placed on the sideboard, was watching him no matter where he was in the dining room. And he wanted to know if he continued watching him even when he, Alex, wasn't looking at him.

"Let's see. Turn around and I'll tell you."

With his infinite confidence in me, Alex immediately turned around.

"Yes, even when you're not looking at him, he's watching you."

"Really? What about you, does he keep watching you even when you're not looking at him?" asked Alex.

"Let's see that too. I'm going to turn around and you tell me if he's watching me."

"No, he's still looking at me," said Alex, as soon as I turned my back.

"So I think that means he's watching you to see if you're misbehaving."

With the face Alex suddenly made and even before he went

crying on Mother's knee, I immediately hurried to console him, telling him that when he had turned around, the photo had only been looking at me. I explained that it was always that way. When a person is looking at the photographer at the moment of being photographed, that's how it is. I even took out the encyclopedia to show him. Almost every page had a famous person on it who was looking at us. He was reassured, but I still feel bad about it. It's become part of these memories.

For Alex, perhaps even more than for me, Mother was the pillar of the family. She was always there, reassuring and protective, and he couldn't image it any other way. At home, the men had only passed through. They were just people we talked about from time to time. Alex said "your father," speaking of mine, whereas I called his Leizer. And the fact that we didn't have the same last name posed no particular problem. I even found it funny when, returning home one day, I found Alex all excited, practically yelling into the phone: "No, not Chigelman! Zygelman, with a Z like Zorro!" and he hung up.

"Who was that?"

"An idiot!"

That's all I could get for an answer, but after that, I think, as if to affirm his identity, Alex had chosen to juggle with his last name in an unusual manner. Instead of spelling out his name in the usual way, specifying each letter with common words or names of reference, he used the names of cities, and preferably foreign cities. I would try to imagine what the person on the other end might be thinking when I would hear Alex say, matter-of-factly, "Zygelman. I'll spell it: Z as in Zagorsk, Y as in Yalta, G as in

Gorlovka, E as in Engels, L as in Leningrad, M as in Moscow, A as in Arkhangelsk, N as in Novosibirsk." Sometimes he changed countries. Other times, because he had made a game of it, he enjoying mixing genres: Z as in zygote bordered Y as in yogurt and G as in grenadine.

Until the day when, having seemingly resolved whatever issue he had, he stopped.

When I speak of Alex, waves of memories whose importance I can barely fathom, flood my mind, unbidden.

Because of his inexhaustible energy, his quick wit, and verbal agility—which made him into a kind of talking Harpo—we long believed he had created a robust system of self-defense. I think we were wrong. Mother resented it when Bubbe said, "Alex isn't like the other children." And yet, even if she didn't mean it as a compliment, Bubbe wasn't entirely wrong.

It was the day Alex returned home from school furious over a composition, even though he had received an excellent grade, that we first had the nagging impression—my mother far more than I—that he wanted to say something, something he couldn't say otherwise, but which we sensed reflected a certain confusion.

His assignment was to "tell an extraordinary story," and Alex told the story of a man in a deep coma, on life support in the hospital with no chance of survival. After a year, against all expectations, he emerges from the coma and asks what day it is.

"Tuesday," the nurse tells him, before she even has a chance to alert the doctor on duty of this miraculous and sudden awakening.

"I slept for four days?" asks the man in astonishment.

"Not exactly," the nurse replies, "a year and four days." The man then pales, opening his eyes wide before closing them forever. The news killed him. Alex had finished his composition by saying that the nurse was his mother and that after the man died she had been dismissed from the hospital for malpractice and that ever since then she had been unemployed. And Alex explained that he now had to watch his pennies, which was why he had been unable to buy the school supplies requested by the school.

Moved by his story and feeling guilty at having punished him, the teacher gave him the best grade in the class.

"I didn't know your mother was a nurse," said the teacher when she called him up to the front to collect his copy.

"She's not a nurse," said Alex, in front of the entire class, "she's a saleswoman in a jewelry store."

"What, she's a saleswoman in a jewelry store? Your story isn't true?"

"No, madame, it isn't true."

"But why did you invent such a story?"

"You told us to invent a story that seemed true."

"But you didn't have to say that your mother was unemployed and to make me think that that was why you didn't buy school supplies. Now I'm sorry I gave you such a good grade."

In telling us the story of his composition, Alex's anger died down, but then he could barely hold back his tears. He had been so proud, he told us, when the teacher announced that he had received the best grade in the class and had even read his text out loud to all the pupils. The humiliation was therefore all the greater. "Even if I had gotten a bad grade, she would have had no right to embarrass me. So why did she have to embarrass me with a good grade?" He was so unhappy that Mother, who must have thought as I did, didn't dare ask him what he had done with the money for his school supplies. But there had to be more to it: he hadn't written this text for nothing, and certainly not simply to justify the money spent elsewhere. Why had he brought Mother into this story and suggested she was unemployed? Why had he solicited the teacher's pity? And why did he say the opposite once he'd received the good grade? Had he unconsciously wanted to express a desire to be heard?

I had too many questions to truly understand what we had seen as just a passing incident. And then, though it didn't clear up the questions, I remembered—feeling it was perhaps not the best moment to mention it—what he had said one night at the dinner table that had made us all laugh: "I'd like to write intelligent things. So intelligent that when I reread them, I won't understand what I wrote."

Stories about Alex keep accumulating in my mind. In particular those in which Bubbe was also present. In the face of his peculiarities, even if she wasn't involved, she generally rolled her eyes as a sign of reprobation. From time to time she threatened another slap. A threat she quickly forgot—or perhaps it's more accurate to say she chose to forget. Except one time.

Since Mother didn't like to leave Alex alone in the house, one evening when she had choir—once a week she practiced with the popular Jewish choir of Paris—and I was out of the house as well, she asked Bubbe to stay with Alex until she got home.

As soon as dinner was over, Alex had wanted to turn on the television. Knowing that Mother didn't want him to watch television at night when he had school the next day, Bubbe firmly opposed this idea. But Alex loved soccer, and that night there was a live broadcast of a match between Juventus of Turin—a team of which Alex was a huge fan—and a French team. In the face of his insistence, Bubbe asked him what was so interesting on television that he was so determined to watch.

"The Juve is on."

"The Jew? What Jew? What's the Jew doing on television?"

"Playing soccer."

Alex's "insolence" was more than she could stand, and as with "Bernard's butt for a lemonade," suddenly there came a slap.

Alex couldn't recover.

Of course he had heard Bubbe say the word "Jew," but he had assumed it was because of her Yiddish accent and he hadn't bothered to correct her. Though he would have been sad not to watch television because of school the next day, he would have consoled himself. But what he couldn't get over, yet again, was a slap for an answer. And again came the tears, springing not out of pain but out of a sense of injustice. This incomprehensible slap, recalling the previous incident, left a scar, a wound that got the better of him. Thus, once in bed, putting off any hope of an explanation, Alex sought only consolation, crying twice as hard upon Mother's return.

Something in him couldn't let it pass. He had to get her back while avoiding a confrontation which he knew he couldn't win. He would get his revenge in another manner. Drawing on his inner resources, his sense of humor, and his playfulness. That was probably why, a few days later, when the four of us—Mother, Bubbe, Alex, and I—were sitting calmly at the table, thinking the tears forgotten, he asked out of the blue:

"Bubbe, how do you say 'Rue des Hospitalières-Saint-Gervais' in Yiddish?"

9

The young woman who had found the photograph of Harpo Marx for me at the Saint-Ouen flea market was named Odile. At the Brasserie Paul-Bert, after eating a portion of fries with our fingers, she told me that she was a researcher. She had come to the flea market looking for a series of illustrated supplements from the *Petit Journal* which a merchant had put aside for her.

Though she had already been loaded up with these supplements, she was drawn nonetheless to the impressive quantity of photographs in which several of us had been digging. She had stopped and was glad she had. Not just for the photo of Harpo Marx that she had brought to my attention, but because she had come across two other photos, one of which was almost a rare find: a postcard from the turn of the century showing the Cherche-Midi military prison. She had been asked to find as many photographs and documents as possible about this prison—slated to be demolished and replaced by a structure that would house the future Maison des Sciences de l'Homme—in preparation for the publication of a history of the building. It was in this prison, she told me, that

Captain Dreyfus was incarcerated after being wrongly accused of treason.

She asked the waiter for some paper napkins to wipe her fingers. I looked over her shoulder. Max still wasn't there; his father, sitting on one of his old armchairs, was hunched over, concentrated on a newspaper spread out on a low table. With a pencil whose tip he regularly wet with his tongue, he seemed to be scrupulously checking off or underlining something, probably something like the horse race entries the next day at Vincennes.

With the table cleared, Odile showed me some issues of the *Petit Journal*, which each Sunday had offered its readers a roundup of the recent news and a full-page colored drawing on its cover.

I leafed through "The Degradation of Alfred Dreyfus," with a helmeted soldier breaking the captain's sword over his knees, "Captain Dreyfus Before the War Council," "The Zola Affair," and the most precious for Odile, the edition of January 20, 1895, titled "Alfred Dreyfus in His Prison," in which Dreyfus is represented as a despairing civilian, leaning against the walls of his cell while a guard, from outside the bars, passes him a mess kit with a chunk of bread.

"He spent nearly three months in this prison before his wife was authorized to visit him," said Odile. "Fortunately, Forzinetti, the officer responsible for the Cherche-Midi prison, who saw Dreyfus daily, was convinced of his innocence. He was the first to say so. He even wrote as much to Lucie Dreyfus and was forced out of the army."

The other photograph that Odile had found wasn't a postcard, but a photograph printed on thick card stock, as was common at the turn of the century and which generally depicted famous

personalities from the political, literary, or artistic worlds, photographed by renowned photographers. It was the portrait of a military man, Lieutenant Colonel Georges Picquart. On the back of
the photo, in meticulous print, was the name of the photographer:
A. Gerschel, 17, Boulevard Saint-Martin.

"17, Boulevard Saint-Martin? Where the André Shoes store is?"

"I don't know if André Shoes are there now," said Odile,
surprised. "Why?" Are you familiar with 17, Boulevard Saint-
Martin?"

"I know the Boulevard Saint-Martin by heart."

"By heart? What do you mean, by heart?"

I replied with the list:

At number 1, La République wine cellar

At number 3, Bally Shoes, Caraud Jewelers

At number 5, Bouquet de la République Bar

At number 7, Tailor

At number 9, Wilson Shoes, Café-Tobacco Store

At number 11, Radio Ciné TSF, La Croix Rose Jewelers

At number 13, Shoes, Galéries Saint-Martin Parfumes

At number 15, Aux Abeilles d'Or, Jewelry-Clocks, Le Record
    du Rire, Jokes, Tricks, and Costumes

At number 17, André Shoes, Daniel Legrand Artificial Flowers

At number 19, Women's Hats, Jewelry

At number 21, Printer

At number 23, Deboucheron Bar, Marcel the Tailor

At number 25, French Clocks, Peuvrier Pharmacy
    Homeopathy

I wouldn't have thought that this listing of shops, which I was
reciting so long after having seen them, read them, heard them,

were still so present in my mind. Odile's eyes almost widened at this outpouring. She had her hand on her mouth as if to stop from interrupting me, and allowed me to continue.

I decided to finish:

At number 27, Koh-I-Nor Jewelers, Thomas Bicycles and Repairs

At number 29, Jewelry-Perfume

At number 31, Book Store-Paper Goods

At number 31B, Le Coucou Cabaret, L'Ambiance Furniture

At number 35, Aux Mines d'Écume, pipes and articles for smokers, Tobias Tailor, Optical Store

At number 37, Restaurant Caillet, Kinérama Cinema

At number 39, Bar-Yton Café-Bar, Comptoir des Grands Boulevards Jewelry, The Good Book Bookstore

At number 41, Post Office

At number 43, Vauguier Photographers

At number 45, La Riviera Café, Rand Brothers

At number 47, Restaurant

At number 49, Renaissance Jewelers

At number 51, Robero Tailor, Universal Stereoscopy

At number 53, Tobacco and Wines, Pharmacy

And at number 55—whew! Cross of Malta Café.

After that, it's the Rue Saint-Martin.

"I'm as exhausted as you are," said Odile, bursting out laughing. "I felt like I was running alongside you down the boulevard. I almost forgot to breathe. But it's incredible that you did that! I can't believe it."

And she called back the waiter to order us drinks.

· · ·

Less than a week later, Odile sent me a letter. She continued the conversation that we had had at the Brasserie Paul-Bert, during which I had been obliged to explain the "Boulevard Game" we had played on Sundays with Leizer. I didn't say much about it. Something held me back. And what had really interested me, in any event, was what it meant to be a researcher. What did it consist of exactly? How did you train for it? Since it seemed too much to explain, Odile chose to give me more of a dictionary definition, telling me basically that a researcher is someone who seeks, who sometimes finds, and then classifies documents with a view to publication or for a public entity. After studying literature she had gone to the National Institute for Documentation Techniques, where she received her diploma as a researcher. You could work full-time for an organization, or freelance on a project basis, and thereby go from subject to subject, from literature to history to art or other subjects. She had chosen the latter option. She promised to tell me more about her work, which she enjoyed, another time. She didn't want to go into it right then and there, the very day we met. And yet, without fully understanding it, what struck me above all about what she did tell me was when she said that the day she realized she had more pleasure in seeking than in finding was the day she realized she had truly become a researcher.

And we exchanged addresses.

The letter from Odile was accompanied by a postcard showing the optician's shop at 37, Boulevard Saint-Martin, where Restaurant Caillet and the Kinérama had been. The photo was captioned "Maison Guilleret, Optician. Furnisher to the Ministries of War and the Navy. 37, Boulevard Saint-Martin, Paris."

"As you probably know," wrote Odile, "today at number 37 are Alexander Clocks and the Bosphorus Cinema."

She began her letter thanking me because upon strolling down the Boulevard Saint-Martin—after my "recitation" she couldn't resist going to see it—she found, at number 29, above the entryway, a plaque celebrating one hundred years since the birth of Méliès. The plaque had been there only a few months, and she recopied the text for me:

GEORGES MÉLIÈS

BORN IN THIS HOUSE

DECEMBER 8, 1861

CREATOR OF CINEMATIC SPECTACLE

MAGICIAN, INVENTOR OF MANY ILLUSIONS

"I was lucky to meet you," she said in her letter. "This recognition of Méliès, though late, is very important for me, because Méliès was a Dreyfusard from the start and made a film on the Dreyfus Affair early on—from the time of the trial in Rennes (1899). The film lasted fifteen minutes—which was unusually long back then—and was banned for a long time, I think due to the obvious sympathy Méliès showed the falsely accused Captain Dreyfus."

And further along, she wrote:

"We should get together again one day—that list of shop names you shot off in rapid succession was like a lesson for me. Although it's not very clear to me, I don't think it's a phenomenon that has to do with memory. To emerge so spontaneously, those names must have been imprinted in you, and—forgive my curiosity—I'd love to know why. But I know I'll have to wait. As you can imagine, I have many questions. And then others I haven't even thought of yet."

As a postscript, Odile promised to seek and to find (she underlined the word "find") other photographs of the Boulevard Saint-Martin.

The letter I wrote in response to Odile's was shorter. Without returning to the issue of shop names—I myself didn't know why I had retained them so well—nor hazarding the issue of questions to come, I picked up on her "forgive my curiosity" because it reminded me of the moment in Truffaut's film when Jim tells Jules the advice his professor gave him, which I recopied for her as I remembered it:

"What should I be in life?"

"A curious person."

"That's not a profession."

"It's not a profession yet. Traveling, writing, learning to live anywhere. The future belongs to the professionally curious."

And I suggested this definition of a researcher to Odile: "A researcher is someone who is professionally curious."

On the way back from depositing my letter in the mailbox on the Rue de Saintonge, I lingered in front of the Winter Circus. My decision came to me in a flash. It was time, if only once, to return home by way of the rooftop.

10

Yes, it was time that I too go home by passing over the roof of the Winter Circus. To take the action I had put out of my mind since that January snow seen from the skylight.

In 1955, the film *Trapeze* was filmed at the Winter Circus. Every day during the months of filming, hundreds of people had gathered outside to catch a glimpse of the stars, while Alex, at barely nine years old, had managed to get inside. On a Winter Circus poster that the clown Zavatta had given to him, he had managed to get the signatures of Gina Lollobrigida, Burt Lancaster, Tony Curtis, and also Carol Reed, the director. Afterward—no doubt beaming with pride—he went to thank Zavatta and to show him the fruits of his perseverance. Zavatta was so impressed he also signed it, writing, "For my friend Alex," and underlining the name "Alex."*

The poster is still tacked above his bed.

•   •   •

*Alex (1897–1983) was also the name of the white clown, Achille Zavatta's regular partner.

As for me, I passed again and again in front of the Circus, delaying my entry, my eyes focused above on the cupola. I drank beverage after beverage at the Circus Bar, a café on the Rue Amelot, hoping for some sort of casual conversation, lingering in front of a photo of the four Bouglione brothers hanging on the wall. I frequented more eagerly, but with no greater success, the little Entrée des Artistes café on the Rue de Crussol, which was less stocked with photographs but was right next to what is, in fact, the artist's entrance to the Winter Circus. Only a few circus hands seemed to stop in the place, in addition to a Spanish-speaking trio whom I assumed to be trapeze artists, based on their physiques.

Every morning I told myself: today's the day.

Sitting with a café crème and a newspaper laid out in front of me in order to justify the length of my stay, I wondered where to begin, how to explain. Should I say that I lived in the Cité Crussol and that twenty years ago my father had snuck into his own house via the roof of the Circus and returned via the same route? Should I explain that he was Jewish and that this had been the best means he could think of to avoid getting caught?

I imagined the discussion:

"Really? So . . . ?"

"And so I'd like to do the same thing."

"But why do you want to go over the Circus roof when you can go home normally?"

"Because I'd like to know how he did it."

"Didn't your father tell you?"

"Well, no, that's the problem. One day he didn't come back. It was in 1942, in July. He must have gotten caught. He was deported and we never saw him again."

"But where were you?"

"I was hidden with my mother and grandmother in Gentilly."

"So why did your father come here if you were living some-where else?"

"Because we'd had to leave very quickly, so he came back to get some important papers, personal things, and he came back several times, I think, because it would have been too dangerous to go this way with his arms full."

"And you haven't asked how he was stopped?"

"Who can we ask? No, we don't know. I suppose that someone saw him on the roof and that he was reported."

"Maybe he was arrested because they thought he was a robber."

"A robber? But they don't deport robbers, they put them in prison."

I would have hated to get into such a discussion. Moreover, in these imaginary conversations, I got confused and was unable to explain the deeper reasons that were prompting me to retrace my father's steps, twenty years after the fact. I would have needed to understand why myself. I knew only that I needed to do it, and that was all. So, counting on the inspiration of the moment, I left this imaginary discussion in suspense.

When I met with a member of the Bouglione family the first words were just about what I had imagined, while the rest of the conversation was of course completely different. I had told myself that the initial introduction was key, and although I got tangled in some preliminary rhetorical precautions, I received a warm welcome.

It wasn't one of the four brothers whose photograph graced

the main wall of the Bar du Cirque. He was younger. There were barely a few years between us.

I don't know if he understood the reasons for my request, but he was sufficiently solicitous to invite me to follow him down a long circular corridor. I could hear the sound of a horse galloping, the repetition strangely evoking the name of the site's owners: Bouglione, Bouglione, Bouglione.

Then, in the wide gap between two red velvet drapes that we passed by, I could see a bareback rider perform an acrobatic routine while standing on two horses galloping side by side around the ring. In a corner, a spiral metal staircase, the narrow confines of which were weakly lit by the exit lights, allowed us to climb onto the roof through a small door. A lock, to which we didn't have the key, prevented us from getting outside. "Wait for me here," said the young Bouglione, "I'll go get the key." In his absence, I had time to read the inscriptions scratched into the wall: "Gino, Olga. An illegible name, 9/14/1946. Kassovic 1953. Dede 1942–1943." And yet other names, sometimes followed by dates, that I ignored. Too recent. Stupidly, as if my father, armed with a penknife, might have taken the time to stop here, I dared to hope to find some trace of a "Jacques," or, even more absurdly, of a "Yankel, 1942." It was ridiculous. Why would he have left a trace when his goal was to avoid leaving any?

"Those are trapeze artists," Bouglione told me, returning with the key. "They come this way for their routines and leave their names and dates as souvenirs."

"How high are we?"

"Twenty-three meters. We're above the Cité Crussol buildings. Shall we go?"

"Let's."

Once I passed through the little wooden door, facing the task that lay before me, I saw only the long line of zinc roofs overhanging the Cité Crussol. I counted the skylights. One, two, three. It was the third, the last. That's where I had to go. Walk to the third skylight, open it, and jump down to the landing, as my father had done. In so doing, I was convinced I would be more complete in some way.

I still hadn't budged from the first slope of the roof where I had been led, with a warning to be careful, not to slip. I felt a kind of peace in hovering there.

On this path, from the spiral stairs to the third skylight, I liked to think that the man who had been my father was taking me by the hand, helping me take my first steps. As if he had been waiting for me and was saying, Look, this is the way I went, just this way.

So, as if he too had needed this moment and was letting go of my hand for the first time, I walked toward the third skylight and imagined him behind me, smiling, encouraging, and confident, and it all seemed easy. Passing the chimneys, my steps overlapped with his, I suddenly felt completely immersed in this undertaking, which I now understood had nothing to do with curiosity.

Later, in what must have been the circus stable, where an employee was conscientiously repainting the gilding in the stalls, we stopped beneath Alexandre, Sampion, Joseph, and Firmin, the four Bouglione brothers, as depicted on a huge color poster. Emilien, who had accompanied me to the roof, was the son of one of them.

Three other posters signed by Gustave Soury, which commemorated major shows, were also hanging on the wall. One of them, illustrated with a particularly impressive drawing, announced "the one and only double human cannonball."

"I was Tony Curtis's double in *Trapeze*," Emilien told me, following my gaze. "I was seventeen."

Like me, he had attended the public school on the Rue Saint-Sébastien. "But I didn't go often. Because we traveled." And the conversation continued.

"How old was your father?"

"Twenty-seven. Why?"

"Because I was thinking of something, but it doesn't work out. It happened later, in '44."

"What happened later?"

"One day, my father told me, in the middle of a show, two German soldiers slipped into the audience and took a guy away—probably a resistance fighter. But since it was at a high point in the show, with the orchestra music, it seems no one realized it. That's why I asked how old your father was, but the guy was older than that. And you say it was in 1942 that he was arrested."

Then he told me that with the overseer's complicity, some Jews and resistance fighters had taken refuge in the circus and were hired as circus hands.

"Did you know that Pipo was Jewish?"

"Pipo, Pipo the clown?"

"Yes, his real name is Sosman. Gustave Joseph Sosman. He comes from a great family of acrobats and horsemen from Belgium and Holland. Like my mother, who was a Van Been. That's why, even within the circus world, no one at the time thought he was Jewish. I think he was the only one worried, because during the occupation, he kept the audiences laughing."

. . .

There were probably other things to say that would have interested me, but that was all he knew. And I left the circus almost regretfully.

Once outside, as I gazed at the cupola with my nose in the air, I realized what I would do when I got home: with the help of the landing ladder, I would open the skylight and look at the path I had just followed an instant earlier, the path my father had taken twenty years before.

11

"What part do I play in this story? The author? An accomplice? A passerby? I am you! That is, any one of you. I am the personification of your desire, of your desire to know everything. People never know more than one side of reality. Why? Because they see only one side of things. But I see all sides . . . because I see in the round. That allows me to be everywhere at once. Everywhere. But where are we here? On a stage. A film set. On a street. We're in Vienna. It's 1900. Let's change our costume. 1900. We're in the past. I adore the past. It's so much more peaceful than the present! And so much more certain than the future! . . ."

So begins *La Ronde*, the Max Ophuls film which I just saw at the Champollion movie theatre.

I remember that at Tarnos we had a real debate with Robert about this film. I didn't take part, as I hadn't seen it. But for those who had seen it—and for whom the subject could be summarized in the fact that a woman meets a man, and that after they make love, the man meets another woman who meets another man and so on—it was shocking. Robert had tried to explain, but not entirely convincingly, that *La Ronde* was really a kind of meditation on the theme of desire and love, and that, despite appearances, it was a very sentimental film.

I had no reason now to put myself in the place of a fourteen-year-old boy and to assess whether I would have judged the film as harshly. Especially since it wasn't the memory of this discussion that interested me today, but the beginning of the film. A beginning which no one had mentioned at the time:

"I adore the past. It's so much more peaceful than the present! And so much more certain than the future! . . ."

Adore the past? What past? In matters of romance, yes, one can adore the past. I had begun to understand this after the screening of *Jules and Jim*, when my mother had given me her arm and spoken about the happy times she'd had in Przytyk with my father and Leizer. And of course, Vienna as well, in 1900, the rounds of love. That past, yes. But the past that came later? The past more certain than the future? Whereas subconsciously I had kept my distance from my childhood—which I was surprising myself by revisiting—I had no desire to relive that past, even if I was now doing my utmost to make it current in order to attempt to understand it.

At school, Alex never responded to his classmates' harassment with "I'll tell my father!" or even with "I'll tell my big brother!" for that matter, because implicitly that would have meant there was no father at home. And since he didn't want to get into any discussions about it, he settled his own accounts. That was how, seeing him come home one day with a serious black eye, before even asking him what had happened, I ended up telling him that he should never let others get the better of him and that he should return blow for blow.

"I know," responded Alex, "but I returned the blow first."

"Alex is an unpredictable boy," a teacher told my mother when he was in fourth grade. Words which my mother, who was more surprised than worried, had relayed to me and which reminded me of Bubbe's remark that Alex was not like the other boys.

Since he did his homework on the dining room table, we saw what he was doing in school. I was intrigued one evening by an odd punishment he had received. He had to recopy a hundred times the words to a patriotic song: "You won't get Alsace and Lorraine, and despite you, we'll remain French." Alex was eager to explain.

During music class, unbeknownst to the teacher, he had been dared by his classmates to sing "You won't get ersatz and Lorraine" instead of "Alsace and Lorraine." What he didn't know was that, at the instigation of the boy standing right in front of him, at the moment the patriot words were to be sung, more than half the class would stop singing.

"Which meant the teacher had no problem hearing 'ersatz and Lorraine,'" continued Alex, "and she saw right away where it was coming from. She said there were some things that you couldn't joke about and she gave me this sentence to copy over a hundred times. Of course, since she's the teacher, she had no choice, but Ridard's the real bastard. He's the one who told the others not to sing."

"So you punched him after school?"

"Not exactly, because Ridard's a big kid who's been held back.

Every time he moves up to the next grade, he has to repeat it. So everyone's afraid of him. But I got a different revenge. Right after recess."

"What did you do?"

"We had geography class with Mr. Ramon, the one we call Ramuntcho, and Ramon asked Ridard what kind of plants grew at the bottom of the ocean. And of course, Ridard didn't know. So I had an idea. Since he sits right in front of me in class, I whispered: 'Carrots!' Ridard hesitated, because he must have thought it was weird that carrots would grow at the bottom of the sea. But then the others, who had also heard me, started whispering: 'Carrots! Carrots!' And Mr. Ramon, who could also hear that there was whispering, but without understanding what we were saying, said, 'We don't whisper!' But then he told Ridard, 'If your ears weren't plugged up, Ridard, you would hear what your friends were whispering to you.' That's what confused Ridard, because it made him think it was the right answer. So he sat up and proudly replied, 'Carrots!' You should have seen Ramuntcho's face. It killed us."

Weeks passed, punctuated with sporadic incidents. Sometimes at school, sometimes elsewhere. One day Alex came home with a black eye, another with a special task as punishment. Then we forgot, but these seeming trifles were resurfacing now. The hazy, unstable past, into which I had avoided delving, was awakening little by little and was now with me all the time.

I wandered the streets more and more, often the same ones over and over. I walked up to Belleville, thinking about what was awakening in me. Learning to proceed mindfully. Not content to take in just the surface. Seeing for myself. Diving down. And in seeking to know what had changed, I remembered Robert pushing the carriage doors open, entering courtyards, in his case seeking to know what hadn't changed.

And I went more and more to the cinema. To the Champollion Theatre, where I had seen *La Ronde*. It was when I saw *Singing in the Rain*, and especially *Les Girls, Les Girls*, that I thought of Leizer's sister who, well before the war, had gone to America in the hope of becoming a music hall dancer, and of Leizer, who had boarded a plane to visit her after twenty years. Then, of course, I thought again of Alex, who like me had learned to live without a father.

What remained unclear, and what I thought about ever since my spontaneous recitation of the Boulevard Saint-Martin shop names and its connection in my mind to Alex's adventures, was the airplane accident of which Leizer was a victim.

I didn't know much, except that it had taken place in October 1949.

My desire to know more was satisfied at the National Library, where I went with the help of Odile.

"Newspapers teach us what we don't remember," she said. "They are waiting for us to read them."

To learn about it, all I had to do was go read about it. Thus I found myself in the newspaper and periodicals room, called the "Oval Room," on the Rue de Richelieu, faced with a pile of the eight daily editions of *France-Soir*, the only French daily which sold more than a million copies, according to its advertising.

Since I was unaccustomed to reading newspapers with articles meant to be read, in principle, on the day of their publication, I had decided to skim through all the successive issues unhurriedly, almost slowly, my only method the turning of pages. Soon, I realized that I was drawn to items that had nothing to do with the topic of my research. As if I were postponing the moment I would find what I was looking for, confident that the information would be waiting for me.

In one case, I decided, from the pile in front of me, which began with the paper dated Saturday, October 1, 1949, to pass directly to the film page—the evening papers were always dated the next day—where I was struck by ads for two films I had never heard of. The first, *Return to Life*, with Bernard Blier, Louis Jouvet, Serge Reggiani, François Perier, and Noël-Noël, had this ad line: "The film that gets applause at every showing." The other was *The Search*, by Fred Zinnemann, with Montgomery Clift—who had just won two Oscars in Hollywood—and its subject was stated as follows: "Escaped from hell, a boy asks an American soldier what a mother is." This ad appeared incongruously beneath a heading that read: IN FIFTEEN MINUTES, YOU'LL KNOW EVERYTHING ABOUT . . . You'll know everything about what in fifteen minutes? About Nazism? About Auschwitz? In fifteen minutes?

What amazed me was that this ad could have been placed beneath such a heading at a moment when time was still conceived of as "postwar" and "prewar." To wit, this ad appeared in the same newspaper: "Just like in prewar days, you can buy a sewing machine at Bon Marché."

On Sunday, October 2, and Monday, October 3:

—Prices lower on butter, but not on bread and meat.

—420,000 elementary school students back to school today.

Wednesday, October 5:

—Tito and his officers: "The USSR is threatening to make war on us, but the Yugoslav army will fight to the end."

—Following Russia, Bulgaria, Hungary, Poland, and Romania, Czechoslovakia breaks its friendship treaty with Yugoslavia.

Since I wasn't trying to keep my distance with respect to what I'd find as I turned the pages, I found myself reading distractedly at first, but then getting interested in various articles. For instance, when I read in the October 7 issue WE'RE MAKING THE ESSENCE OF NAZISM OUR OWN, AFFIRMS THE DRP, A RIGHT-WING GERMAN PARTY, I was sorry I hadn't brought writing materials in order to jot down items of interest. I did so the next day, showing up that morning equipped with paper and carefully sharpened pencils. Once I was seated, I recognized some faces from the day before, bent over articles that at the time had been meaningful enough to print. Their confident movements and gestures reminded me that I was a newcomer there.

Turning the pages deliberately, I returned to the issues from Saturday, October 8, right where I had left off.

—"On the Carrousel Bridge, in the middle of the night, René told the taxi driver to stop, threw himself into the Seine and drowned right in front of the woman who had just refused his hand in marriage."

The next day, there was nothing on this item. Sometimes you want to know more. How they met. What they did for a living. What the woman was thinking after she yelled, "No, don't!" as the man who loved her was disappearing in the waters of the Seine.

What would become of her? "That's life," as Monsieur Victor would say, folding his *France-Soir*.

Also on Saturday, October 8, appeared:

—A wave of arrests in Czechoslovakia. Nearly 6,000 "opponents" rounded up in the last three days.

—Rush to the west: 20,000 Germans pass through the Iron Curtain.

—The release of *Bitter Rice* with Sylvana Mangano.

—Wrestling at the Winter Circus.

Sunday, October 9 and Monday, October 10:

—Under the heading IN FIFTEEN MINUTES, YOU'LL KNOW EVERYTHING ABOUT . . . : the elections in Austria: 430,000 amnestied Austrian neo-Nazis (out of 536,000) vote tomorrow for the first time.

Tuesday, October 11:

—Austria: the neo-Nazis obtain 10 percent of the seats. Hitler's birthplace votes right.

—Czechoslovakia: the purification campaign includes 50,000 arrests.

—*The Bicycle Thief* chosen film of the year for 1949, third month of triumph at the Biarritz and the Madeleine.

Tuesday, October 12:

—Jules Moch determined to form a new government.

Thursday, October 13:

—Rajik (former foreign minister of Hungary) in the final court of appeal. The accused are not present at the trial, as per the law.

Friday, October 14:

—Nothing particularly notable.

Saturday, October 15:

    —Jules Moch voted in with 311 votes (constitutional major-
       ity: 310 votes).

Sunday, October 16 and Monday, October 17 . . .

And then, I'd had enough. I must not be cut out for taking
notes on everything the newspaper tells me. Since this was all on
my own account, since I wasn't answering to anyone, why was
I persisting in dwelling on items that were important, no doubt,
but to others. What was this information teaching me? These
events, these printed facts, did nothing for me. Why pull them
out of oblivion when I didn't know what to do with them? Even
gathered together, they didn't form a memory.

Of course, it's true that, projected back into the heart of that
October, I had learned that France had had no government for
a month. Jules Moch had given up. As had Queuille a few days
before. As would René Mayer a few days later, even though he had
been voted in with 341 votes versus 183. As would Georges Bidault
later still. I had also learned about the scandal of the hanging of
Laszlo Rajik, forty-eight hours after he was condemned to death.
And equally abject, the liberation by the Americans of Ilse Koch,
known as "the bitch of Buchenwald." A photo showed her smiling
at the exit to her prison.

On the entertainment page, they announced the release of
Jeanne d'Arc with Ingrid Bergman, and of *The Third Man* with Orson
Welles, which won the Grand Prix at the Cannes Film Festival,
and the second month of triumphal success of *Return to Life*. But
I had come for something else.

So, fearing my eyes would tire and lose the determination of the first day, I allowed them to skim from one item to another. Impatiently.

And there it was. In the special edition of *France-Soir* dated Saturday, October 29, 1949. On the first page. Over eight columns.

BOXING CHAMPION MARCEL CERDAN'S PLANE
(PARIS–NEW YORK) DOWN IN THE AZORES
WITH 48 PEOPLE ABOARD

There were survivors. The final minutes: at 1:20 PM the following radio message was transmitted from the Azores to Air France: "Plane F.B.A.-Z.N. found Pic Algarvia (the Azores) situated North East Sao Miguel—Stop—Rescue plane says there may be survivors—Stop—Heading there."

So Leizer was on Cerdan's plane?

In the following edition of *France-Soir*, at the end of the article which covered practically the entire first page, a last-minute text box gave the following message: "Plane found burned—Stop—No survivors." And at the bottom, "List of Passengers on page 5."

Yes, there they were, on page 5, and putting off reading the article, I looked to find Leizer's name among the forty-eight names presented in a list, followed by their year of birth, their nationality, and their profession.

John Abbati, born 1895, American, without profession.

Mustapha Abdoumi, born 1923, farmer in Lebanon.

Hanna Abboud, born 1928, without profession, Syrian.

Eghline Askkan-Ebrahimi, born 1915, without profession,
Tehran.

Joseph Aharony, born 1904, Israeli, lawyer.

Jean-Pierre Aduriz, born 1926, French farmer, in the Aldudes
(lower Pyrénées).

Only when I got to the name of Marcel Cerdan (Marcel Cerdan,
born 1916, boxer, Casablanca) did I realize that the list of names
was in alphabetical order. To find Leizer's name, I had to skip to
the bottom, to the last line:

Lazare Zygelman, born 1915, undetermined nationality, tailor, 7 Rue Oberkampf, Paris.

How was it that I didn't know that Leizer was on Cerdan's
plane? Why? At the age of nine, I must have already known who
Cerdan was. And at school, the accident must have been discussed.
I know that for several days my mother had kept me home from
school. Had she made this choice to protect me? Had she said
something to the teacher, fearing that the children would talk
about Cerdan's death? At home, as is customary after a death,
the radio must have been turned off and the newspapers carefully
hidden. And for me to have remembered only Leizer's death, this
event must have been forgotten by the time I returned to school,
after the All Saint's Day vacation.

Thus it had taken me thirteen years to discover Leizer's name
in the paper. And since I couldn't just walk out of the National
Library and leave it there, and perhaps because I had been kept
in the dark about everything I had just learned, I copied almost
everything down.

It was true: newspapers are there also to teach us what we don't remember. But then what? By recopying it, do we revive an event? At most, by retrieving it from time's passing, we avoid losing it entirely. But to do what with it? What should be done with these discoveries, and this brand new knowledge?

I had just spent two days looking in newspapers for evidence of the airplane accident that had caused Leizer's death. He wasn't somewhere at the bottom of the ocean, as my mother had told me when we left the movie. He had been reduced to ash. It was written in the editions dated Sunday, October 30, and Monday, October 31. My mother must have known that. And it must have been hard for her to forget it. To accept that he too had been burned to ash. I remembered her words: "Leizer was the same way. I had told him to go by boat, that it was safer, but he didn't want to listen. He said he'd be back sooner this way. So he bought a plane ticket and didn't even get to see his sister in America, where she was waiting for him."

Aside from that evening, my mother never spoke of Aunt Esther. As a result, Alex didn't either. Even though it was his aunt. An aunt whom I imagined as an adolescent, arriving on Broadway, learning tap, and attending auditions. An aunt whom I imagined today, living alone in New York, her only family a nephew in Paris with whom she may not have dared get in touch. I didn't resent her for having probably influenced Leizer's decision to take the plane. Unlike my mother, who, I think, couldn't help blaming her still.

So I wrote a long letter to Esther Zygelman. The reply, which was also long, arrived in short order.

12

Dear Bernard,

I have a packet of letter paper in front of me, and my hand holding the pen, which I just filled with ink, is shaking before I even start writing the first word. Shaking just as it did the day when I opened the envelope that contained your letter, which I have been carrying around with me ever since.

I have been waiting for a letter from Paris for so long. Of course you may wonder why I didn't write myself. I did in the beginning. For Rosh Hashanah. Three years in a row. But I never got an answer. It's true that they weren't really letters. Just a signature beneath a preprinted text on the back of a postcard. But I didn't dare write more. I knew that Hannah, your mother, blamed me for having Leizer fly. So I stopped writing and all I could do was cry because I had no family anymore. Life is strange—now I'm crying because I just found one. And just so you know, next to the letter paper I'm writing on I also placed a tissue, ready to serve.

Now, since you asked me many questions, I'll start my story from the beginning.

I was born in 1916, a year after Leizer. And even as a little girl, I would have wanted to marry him if he hadn't been my brother, I admired him so much. Maybe that is why I never married. I don't think so, but I'll tell you about that later.

In 1929, one of my mother's brothers visited from America. His name was Max, but when we spoke of him we always called him "our American uncle," because we knew he'd become rich. So of course, after he had distributed the gifts and visited the neighbors, we asked him lots of questions. Especially Leizer and I.

He had left in 1918, just after World War I, and was taken in by a cousin who had a dairy shop in New York. Before anything else, right upon his arrival, this cousin brought him to the roof of his building. There, he opened my uncle's suitcase and emptied its contents over the city from eight stories up. And while the Polish shirts drifted over the streets of New York, he told him: "Now we'll go buy you a brand new suit, and you'll be like a real American." After that, he brought him into his business, which they called "The New York Butter-and-Eggs Store"—"Service with a Smile" was their slogan. And that's how they got rich.

But this Uncle Max had a passion which he spoke to us about with far more enthusiasm than his butter-and-eggs business: the Broadway dance halls and cabarets. He took a special pair of shoes from his suitcase and on the wood floor of the dining room, he did a tap dance. I was dazzled.

Thanks to him, two weeks later, I was the one who did a tap dance on the kitchen table.

"Golda," my uncle told my mother, "your daughter is going to be a great dancer." But when he added, "She should come with me to America," my mother nearly fainted.

For several days, that's all we talked about. You could see that my father was torn up, but he buried himself in his work and said nothing. My mother, who agreed I was a gifted dancer—what mother wouldn't have agreed?—didn't see why I shouldn't have a dance career in Poland. "Because America is the best place to get paid to be a dancer, America is a better place," said my uncle. "The word 'dollar' has a better ring than the word 'zloty.' Who ever heard of a zloty once you pass the border?" My mother agreed with this as well, even if she thought I was a little too young. Not too young to earn a living, but to leave the family, even though all around us many families had been separated by the ocean.

But Max, my uncle, was persistent. He said that unlike in Poland, in New York a talented Jew could have a bright future. And he cited Irving Berlin, who had started as a singing waiter, and who all of Broadway was now falling over, and Gershwin, and Fanny Brice, and Al Jolson, and many others of whom neither my mother nor anyone in my family had heard, and he started singing "Swanee, how I love you, how I love you, my dear old Swanee" with the Yiddish accent he never lost. And when my mother had only her tears left to counter his arguments, she ended up letting herself be convinced.

A few weeks later, from the bridge of a ship belonging

to the Red Star Line, I caught a glimpse of the Statue of Liberty.

I had intended to leave out the story of my departure for fear that tears would come thinking about it, but it's too late. During the crossing, I could see my mother's face crying on the dock, and I thought of the song "A Brivele der Mamen." You know: "Mayn kind, mayn treyst, du forst avek."* She was afraid she'd never see me again. Thanks to Hitler, she was right. And to sum up it all up, now I'm the one who's crying.

Upon my arrival in New York, Uncle Max had me take English classes, then dancing and singing classes.

And then one day, he told me, "Esther, we need to find a job for you where you can meet all types of people." And that's how I ended up at Katz's Delicatessen on the Lower East Side, at the age of almost fifteen.

When I thought about the fact that Irving Berlin had been a singing waiter when he was fifteen, and I learned that he was born in 1888, the year Katz's opened, I saw it as a sign of fate.

He had proven that an immigrant from Siberia, the son of a cantor, just like Al Jolson, could be the author of "God Bless America," a song that is sung by millions of Americans. So with a smile and a few tap steps, I served the regulars at Katz's platters of Keiss Kichen, which here we call cheese-cake. It's true you meet all types of people there. People from the garment industry, and people from the Yiddish theater, to whom I served bowls of chicken soup with kneidlech.

*"My child, my comfort, you are leaving."

I only had to be careful that the men, and not only the single men, kept their hands in their pockets.

You didn't stay a waitress at Katz's for long. It was a place of transition while you waited to find something else. Usually a husband. Because at the end of the day, it's good to have a man of your own who speaks nicely to you. If he's rich, all the better. Over a glass of tea the would-be husbands talked with the mothers, who didn't take any nonsense, and sometimes the exchange of words ended in a marriage, followed at times by the provision of a food subsidy.

But I wanted a different kind of life, and I found work at the Yiddish theater on Irving Place, directed by Maurice Schwartz. Maurice Schwartz was looking for dancers who spoke Yiddish, since he was planning to put together a musical comedy by Abraham Goldfaden and take it on tour around the United States. The tour lasted several months. If you want to know what it was like to tour with a troupe of actors, performing almost every night in a different city throughout the United States, read the biography of Harpo Marx, *Harpo Speaks!*, which was published here last year. Not only is it beautifully written, but even now that I've left the stage I continue to read long passages because I learn as much about life as about theater.

My feeling is that theater is the representation of life, and that life has two sides: good and bad. And if you want to grapple with it, you should look to the good side. But without ever forgetting that the bad side isn't far off.

It was in looking to the good side that I discovered the existence of the Marx Brothers. Uncle Max had taken me to see *Animal Crackers* at the movie theater, but I hadn't been in America long enough to understand all the dialogue. That's probably why Harpo, the brother who never said a word, caught my attention. I understood English much better one year later, when *Monkey Business* came out. There again, I could only see one actor—he was twice my age, but even when he was chasing a blond across the screen he kept the spirit of a child. That day, I felt something I had never felt before: that my eyes and heart would forever be open to him.

They were still open when, ten years later, in 1941, I was one of the dancers chosen to appear in a long musical sequence for the film *The Big Store*, which Metro-Goldwyn-Mayer was producing with the Marx Brothers as stars. But Harpo, who was as sweet at work as on the screen, was married to the actress Susan Fleming and no longer ran after blonds.

After the attack on Pearl Harbor, the United States entered the war, and Harpo wanted to enlist immediately. But he was considered too old to wear a uniform, so he decided to fight as an actor. And again, I was fortunate to be one of the fifteen chorus girls he chose to form a troupe, and for four years we performed on military bases, naval bases, and in hospitals, for the benefit of our soldiers.

But I have to back up a bit, to the time when I arrived in New York. At that time, my uncle introduced me to everything that mattered on Broadway, which he considered indispensable to my artistic education. That was how I ended up seeing performances by Al Jolson, Fanny Brice, Ethel Merman, and Sophie Tucker, the names he had mentioned when he came to see us in Przytyk. I remember the first big show he took me to see as if it were yesterday. It was *Girl Crazy* by Gershwin at the Alvin Theater, with Ethel Merman and Ginger Rogers.

I also remember the first years, at night, when my uncle and I would walk on Broadway, where the names of the kings and queens of the New York stage shone in huge, brightly lit letters, and my eyes would shine as well, imagining myself on the stage waving at the cheering audience.

My name never appeared in bright lights outside the theaters. Of course, like thousands of other girls who already in the days of Ziegfeld were looking to work on Broadway, I had hoped to play a great role one day, the starring role, before playing my final role: six feet under, eyes forever shut, with worms your only partner. And yet, from audition to audition, with hard work and perseverance, and also, I think, a little talent, I became what they call "one of the girls men like to watch."

So, like the others, I received gifts. Chocolates at first, then pins, bracelets, necklaces. Bouquets of flowers awaited me in my dressing room, offered by men who, after taking off their wedding rings, would invite me out to dinner. And maybe it was because of those gifts that I never thought of looking for a husband. Does a devoted wife get that many gifts? When her husband's at work and the children at school, when she has dusted everywhere and the house is clean, who can she talk to? The walls?

In any case, I've always loved dancing for an audience. Even if you start to wonder when you see men looking at you with binoculars from the first row. If it's just to study our beauty marks, orchestra seats are a little expensive.

And then comes the day when, after taking off your makeup, you look at yourself for a long time in the mirror—you must have seen this scene a thousand times in film—and you look around and you see what you refused to see for some time: the flowers, whose presence in your dressing room were so reassuring, are no longer there to welcome you. I told myself at that point that it was time to do other things. So, with no food stipend, after a final season at Radio City Music Hall dancing to the tunes of Cole Porter, I sold all my jewelry, with no regrets, and bought myself a flower shop. It's not far from Radio City Music Hall, but the distance that separates me from the stage is a more reasonable one.

I can't claim that making bouquets of flowers is as thrilling as receiving them, but at least now I see the morning sun and I can sing "Good Morning" at an appropriate hour. And most of all, even if there is nothing particularly exciting about watering flowers, I'm a lot less nervous watering them than I was when I was called in for auditions.

That's the whole story. At least what I can convey in a letter. More than this would be a novel, one of those novels in which you say everything you know.

Now that I rediscovered a family, I hope it won't be too long before I receive another letter from you. Even though, ever since I heard Arthur Sheekman saying that he caught Harpo Marx one day responding to a letter he had received five years earlier, I know that a lack of response can be very innocent. Do you have a photograph of yourself? Of Alex?

I would love to know what kind of boy he is. And I would love to hold him in my arms.

Kisses to all three of you,
Your Aunt Esther

P.S. As you requested, I am enclosing a photo of myself. As you can see, it's not a recent photo—it's a really old one, I must have been eighteen at the time. It's one of those I used to send to theater directors. If I sent you one surrounded by my flowers, you might wonder how as a chorus girl I managed to boost the morale of our troops during the war.

13

How beautiful our Aunt Esther was, with her slit skirt, at eighteen!

Her photo is now tacked above Alex's bed. Right next to the poster from Zavatta. It was his by right.

He couldn't keep still when he learned that his aunt had played in a film with Harpo Marx. He couldn't stop turning in circles, as if he had diarrhea or a toothache.

He had caught the Marx bug as a child when he saw *The Big Store* at the theater, and he had never been cured. *The Big Store* was the very film in which Esther, his aunt, his father's sister, had appeared. And what's more, she also loved Harpo best of all the Marx Brothers. He reproached me for not having written to her sooner, and because he wanted to know more, he demanded that I respond almost immediately. Suddenly regretting that he hadn't worked on his English enough in school to be able to write to her himself—he was in ninth grade—he was ready to do anything, even enroll in Berlitz, to catch up. He would have taken the plane that instant to go see his aunt in New York, but he kept his desire to himself, waiting for a more opportune moment to speak about it.

I found some photos of Alex and myself. Recent photos. And

since I didn't know what pictures she had of Leizer, thinking that it would make her happy, I also had a copy made of the one in which he is with my father, sitting in the grass.

In awaiting these reproductions, I had time to think about what Esther apparently cared about most: hearing about Alex.

Telling her about their common love of Harpo was a no-brainer, and Alex had already instructed me to write about it. And then I thought about what we called in the family "the frog story."

It was when Bubbe was still alive. That day, Mother returned from work and found herself in the middle of an argument. "Bubbe is anti-Semitic against the frogs!" Alex was yelling. First, Mother explained to him that you could only be anti-Semitic against Jews. Having until that point heard this word only from Bubbe's mouth, Alex had thought that it was a generic term for someone who doesn't like others. Human or animal. And since he was holding something in the palms of his hands, closed like a shell, something visibly precious, Mother asked to see it. "It's a baby frog," Alex said. "It was in the salad and Bubbe wanted to throw it in the garbage." He had heard Bubbe scream while he was doing his homework in the dining room, and he had run in just in time to see her trying to get rid of it, disgusted.

I arrived at the moment when Alex was telling how he had saved the frog from certain death, and I advised him, if he wanted to keep it alive, to put it in a jar. While Bubbe shrugged her shoulders, Mother found a glass salad bowl in which I put a little water. "I'll give him my portion," said Alex, when he saw me adding two lettuce leaves. After which, very delicately, he deposited his frog, which was barely three centimeters long, on one of the leaves.

During dinner, Alex didn't take his eyes off the salad bowl

on the sideboard. He was both happy—the frog had found a place to live—and worried—"he must be looking for his mother everywhere."

"His mother must also be looking everywhere for him," said Mother, moved. "It would be best to put him back in his natural habitat." She wisely suggested bringing him the next day to the botanical garden. Thus the next morning, a Sunday, my mother and I—with Alex two steps ahead holding the salad bowl in his hands, a piece of paper with holes affixed to the top to allow the frog to breathe—found ourselves walking through the alleys of the botanical garden in search of a groundskeeper. One of them had told us that near the entrance to the menagerie were several swampy basins, where Alex soon had the joy of seeing several other batrachians frolicking. He loved to watch them standing immobile for a long time and then suddenly disappearing beneath the duckweed. There was something unpredictable about their movements that fascinated him.

The groundskeeper who had directed us had assured us we would find specialists ready to help us near the basins. There were two, with caps on their heads, chatting. One of them, drawn in by the salad bowl, perhaps suspecting some type of kidnapping, approached us.

"It's a baby frog," said Alex immediately, drawing back the perforated paper.

"No, it's not a baby anymore," said the man kindly, "it's almost an adult. You see, it's lost its tail. It's only going to grow one or two centimeters more at most. What do you want to do with it?"

"We want to put it back in its natural habitat," responded Alex, using Mother's words.

"That's a good idea. Come, you can put it in a pond yourself where there are other green frogs."

Which he did, convinced by this man's argument that life together with his fellow frogs would be less monotonous than life in a salad bowl with no future.

And it was only after learning that frogs can hop more than twenty times their size, that they live an average of a dozen years, and especially that he could come visit it, that Alex agreed to leave. On our way out we passed by the botanical garden bookstore to buy him a book on frogs, the cover of which showed a green frog consuming a blue dragonfly.

That was the story I told Esther. I told it as best I could. Others muscled their way in or came to mind by association, or simply because Alex was their protagonist, but it seemed to me, at least initially, that this story of the frog described him best.

Dear Bernard,

What a shock it was to receive Alex's photo. When I told you that when I received your first letter I felt I had found a family, I didn't know how true that was. Now, with his photo next to me, I know it for sure. How can a son resemble his father so much? Alex is exactly the same age as Leizer was when I left Poland and it's as if I was seeing him again after all this time, his face unmarked by the passing years. Even though he was already working with our father, Leizer and I were still children, and during those first years we wrote to one another a great deal. We had so much to tell each other. Except for the advice. Leizer wrote it but it was

my mother dictating. Until the day when I stopped hearing
from them. The day the Germans invaded Poland. But you
know all that.

When I speak about family, I'm speaking about the one
I left, because here in America, there was my uncle, who took
such good care of me. But with him, it's not the same. He
found his grave at the end of his days, where I lay three stones
on Yom Kippur. He died three years ago, at the age of sixty-
five. He had married late, with a former Ziegfeld Follies girl,
whom he met at Lindy's, where she had become a waitress.
Lindy's was another delicatessen, famous for its cheesecake
and gefilte fish, but not only. Until dawn you could see all of
Broadway there, stars and celebrities, as well as more ques-
tionable characters: professional card sharks, bookies, or
gangsters. For Lucy, Max was the perfect husband. For her,
he spent without counting. She wore rings and bracelets, as
in the days of her splendor. But of course, they had no future
plans together, the way you do when you're twenty years old.
They lived day-to-day and were happy that way, and they
hoped it would last a bit longer than it did. With Lucy on
his arm, Max was as happy and proud as the day he put on
his first suit from the Milgram Brothers, and with her, his
nights were even sweeter.

When he got sick, Lucy was a model wife. Devoted, at-
tentive, always there for him. She was the one to close his
eyes, because until the end, he saw only her.

After Max's death, Lucy and I saw each other quite often.
She shared her experience with me.

"So long as I was kicking high, I didn't see any point in

marrying, whereas that's exactly when you should do it. You can have your pick. And then, you should always ask yourself if anyone would miss you if you left the stage. The day I counted up my friends in the world of entertainment and realized that no one in that world would miss me was the day I left and became a waitress at Lindy's, where I had some family. And then Max came along, and thanks to him, I experienced everything a woman should experience in life."

And ever since, Lucy has hoped I would meet a man, who might come into my store for a reason other than offering flowers to one of the girls still kicking high on the other side of the avenue.

But I'm not complaining. I live a tranquil life. And since your letters from the other side of the ocean, I know there's a family living in France that I belong to. When I hear that Harpo Marx is Alex's favorite actor, it's as if he is doubly my nephew. And since he wants to hear the latest about the Marx family, tell him that unfortunately Chico died last year, at the age of seventy-four, that Groucho is still the host of a television show, and that Harpo has retired with his family to Palm Springs. Tell him I will send him a package with the memoir that Harpo just published. It's written in simple, straightforward language that will allow him to make good progress in English.

Now to answer your other questions.

Yes, I was in another film, *The Great Ziegfeld*. But you wouldn't be able to recognize me in that one either. There are too many people. It's a film that was shot with a big budget and received three Oscars in Hollywood. I was very well paid. Much better than in the theater, but as I've already said, I loved performing and dancing for a live audience best of all. I even danced for audiences that stood up at the end of the performance and threw their hats in the air, because as you may know, in America, hats are also used to show your pleasure. Whereas on a film set, as soon as the technicians hear the word "Cut!" they move on to the next scene, and that's that.

You also asked me who Sophie Tucker is. Since you mentioned the American singers you like, listen to Judy Garland and then Bessie Smith. Then imagine a voice that would be right between the two and you'll have a good idea of what Sophie Tucker sounds like. If I were to write you how she sings "A Yiddishe Mama" (which she always sings in Yiddish before singing it in English), this letter would be soaked with tears. I have the record at home, but I haven't listened to it in several years. I can't. It's carefully tucked away, and it's better that way. Sophie Tucker, whose real name was Sonia Kalish, was born in Russia in 1884, but she sings "The Man I Love" or "After You've Gone" as if she were "Made in Harlem." Lucy, who was in one of her shows, told me that Sophie Tucker liked to say about girls in show business: "From birth to eighteen years old, she needs good parents. From eighteen to thirty-five, she needs a good body. From thirty-five to fifty-five, she needs money." And having been a vaudeville actress from the age of twelve, she would add: "I've been rich and I've been poor. Believe me, rich is better."

You asked me if I planned to come to Paris one day. What can I say? Yes, of course, I'd love to. But it's still too soon to think about it. And who would water my flowers when I'm gone?

Anyway, why don't you and Alex come here? I could finally hold you to my heart, and you'll see that since I stopped dancing, there's plenty of room there.

Well, my hands are tired so I'll stop here. One was holding the pen, the other my handkerchief.

Kisses to you, my dear Bernard, and don't forget to kiss Alex and your mother for me.

—Aunt Esther

P.S.: What a beautiful story about the green frog! All my friends are talking about it.

14

"If you want, you could take Bubbe's room," my mother told me.

That was a year ago. The twenty-four-hour candle that commemorated the first anniversary of my grandmother's death had just gone out. I've slept there ever since, just as Bubbe had done since shortly after Alex's birth.

I was still in bed when I heard someone knocking at the door. It was Alex, telling me that a Mr. Giraud had telephoned for me.

"He left his number. You'll find it near the telephone," Alex told me through the door. "I'm going to the pool."

I had met Robert Giraud at Chez Moineau, a cabaret on the Rue Guenegaud.

Ever since the film shoot, I would go to this cabaret from time to time to hear Florencie sing. Florencie had had a small role in *Jules and Jim* the same day as I had.

When I went there for the first time, I didn't know if he would recognize me. And then, starting with Aristide Bruant's "A la bastoche," when he sang, "His mother, who had no husband / called him her li'l Henry / but others called him the pickpocket / of the

Bastille," when he turned toward me with the hint of a smile as if to acknowledge me, I wondered exactly what we had talked about the day of the shoot.

To the songs by Bruant that I associated with him, he had added some songs by Gaston Couté, the antiwar poet and songwriter who wrote "La Chanson du gas qui a mal tourné." Following which, after sipping some wine, he sang "Où est-il donc?" the song that Fréhel sang in *Pépé le Moko*. Then, once he put his guitar away, he ordered another wine and came to sit near me, and we chatted a bit.

Robert Giraud also went fairly regularly to spend the evening at Chez Moineau. One night, he pulled himself away from the bar, a glass of red wine in his hand, and came to sit at our table. Florencie introduced us. I already knew Giraud's name from having seen it in writing in *Paris insolite*, by Jean-Paul Clébert. The book was dedicated to him as well as to Robert Doisneau, the photographer. Speaking of Giraud, whom he called Bob, Clébert had written that he was the greatest expert on social fantasy in Paris. The half-amused, half-disturbed glance he made at my fruit juice made me hesitate to clink glasses with him, and I realized that without the friendly presence of Florencie, we might never have met.

Robert Giraud liked stories. "My vice is my love of stories," he would say.

A listening specialist, he was always available, one elbow on the bar; he loved firsthand stories, stories told by those who claimed to have lived them—for many people often claimed the same stories as their own, he would say. He could never resist the pleasure of a conversation and he used all his senses to take in everything around him—you could only hope to follow him wherever he went, looking and listening with close attention.

Once Giraud left, Florencie told me that he had been the one who had inspired him to sing Fréhel.

"Giraud met Fréhel in Fréhel's final years. In her final months even. He and a friend of his, Pierre Merindol, who was a journalist and maybe even a former philosophy professor, had discovered an old accordion bar on the Rue du Cardinal-Lemoine that hadn't been touched, its walls still painted in the red of the time. The tables and benches were still attached to the floor because of fights. At the beginning, with three musicians perched on a platform, people would dance. It wasn't an open-air café or dance hall, like the place your friend found in Belleville, it was more for Saturday nights than for Sunday afternoons, but it attracted a lot of people and everyone was happy. One day, to liven things up, they decided to go see Fréhel and they didn't have much trouble convincing her to come sing. She was holy, Merindol said, and when he talks about her, Giraud always calls her "the great Fréhel.""

"What became of that accordion bar?"

"It closed. I think business was good, but I think I heard that the owners had some kind of dealings with the underworld and one day the place was closed. But it's been over ten years, since Fréhel died in '51."

Ever since then, I would head to Chez Moineau not only to see Florencie, but also to see Robert Giraud. "In a bistro, I don't have to talk," he would say, "only listen."

Giraud warehoused stories. He collected them from café to café, and dialogued with them internally to keep them alive. Then he, in turn, told these stories. But better. You can find them in Le Vin des Rues, a book he wrote a few years ago. Thanks to which, they'll last longer than those who told them.

I usually left Chez Moineau a little after midnight, sometimes with Giraud, who would finish off the night at Les Halles, and together we would cross the Seine at Pont-Neuf. I would then hurry to Le Châtelet to catch the last metro, which I sometimes missed. If that was the case I would return home on foot, via the Rue de Rivoli, the Rue Vieille-du-Temple, the Rue des Filles-du-Calvaire. Or Rue des Archives, to Rue des Francs-Bourgeois and the silence of the Place des Vosges to vary the route.

It was at the Café de la Poste, not far from Le Châtelet, that Robert Giraud often headed next. Sometimes I would tag along, deliberately missing my train. The long bar of the Café de la Poste functioned like an employment agency: those who awaited the trucks, with their crates of fruit and vegetables, could earn a few francs or pick up two or three heads of cauliflower and a bunch of leeks in exchange for unloading the goods and piling up the crates. Giraud had done that long ago with Fifi the Gypsy, a character about whom he spoke often.

"There is no better place for a loner than a bistro," Giraud would say, taking it upon himself to order two glasses of red wine. "Because your ears always hear something you can comment on and make a connection. But then, you need to come back. Because it's better to have a drink in a place where they know your name. You're more at ease. But there are also some people you never see again. They're there for a time, in the same place, and then one day they never show up again. Off somewhere else. Erased. All you remember is what everyone called them."

The telephone number Robert Giraud gave me was the number of the Corona, a big café on the Quai du Louvre, opposite his wife's book stall. In the interest of enlightening me, he was inviting me to an unusual spectacle the next day, Sunday, and asked me to meet him at the Canon d'Or, Rue Lecuyer, at the gate to the Saint-Ouen flea market.

At the Canon d'Or, the conversation hardly varied from the talk that was usual inside the walls of Paris. With the site-specific distinction that chatter inevitably focused on what was being bought and sold outside.

"Let's go see the show," said Giraud, after a glass of wine and a few handshakes.

While he might vary the order of his stops within a given perimeter, Giraud never changed his circuit. And he was amazed, when he happened to watch television, at people's need to travel to the ends of the earth when there was so much to discover right nearby. "There is always, everywhere, a house specialty or attraction that is worthy of special attention," he would say.

We walked side by side toward the café where an attraction awaited me, the nature of which he refused to reveal. The café wasn't far: Rue du Plaisir, Pleasure Street, the location of which I would soon learn was quite appropriate.

"Here we are," said Giraud, pushing open the door.

"We were waiting just for you to get started," said Mr. Blaise, the owner of the place.

The locking of the door right after our arrival announced that the café was "full" and at the same time suggested something enigmatic, secret, bordering on clandestine.

The café was rectangular, with the counter situated not near the back, as is often the case, but on the left. All the tables had been pushed to the right.

In between the counter and the tables, opposite a man in work clothes, nearly fifty people were seated with their backs to the wall in three rows, like a choir ready for a concert. This very particular clientele, dressed in such a well-to-do manner that one wondered how they had ended up here, was almost entirely female.

"I am going to ask the kind audience for a little silence so that our Monsieur Raymond might begin," said Monsieur Blaise, laying his hand on the shoulder of the man standing alone. "I would also ask the ladies and gentlemen to kindly refrain from taking any photographs."

The silence obtained, Monsieur Blaise went behind the counter and returned with a metal pail filled with two liters of water. He had the ladies in the first row, for whom he had moved up some chairs, confirm the contents, and then placed the bucket at the feet of the man, Monsieur Raymond, who still hadn't said a word.

To each his role.

"Let's stay near the entrance," Giraud said, leaning his elbows on the counter, "that's where we can best see what there is to see."

Intrigued, with no idea what there was to see except something unexpected, I stayed by the door. I was a bit surprised since from the door you could see Monsieur Raymond only from the back. And I was utterly stupefied when Monsieur Blaise, still speaking to the audience, asked for one or two volunteers to lift their skirts.

Two women, who showed no sign of surprise, spontaneously rose from their seats and immediately did as asked, soon followed by a third. And by two others still. And very quickly, without even being asked as much, in copycat fashion, panties appeared. White and pink. Some decorated with lace. One of these ladies, the last to stand up from her seat, not knowing what to do with her purse, handed it to a man, probably her husband, who inside must have been sweaty with confusion.

That was when Monsieur Raymond dropped his pants. And standing there, his pants down, cap firmly on his head, his shirt barely hiding the nudity of his buttocks, arms to the side, he bent his knees for a brief instant and stood up slowly, accompanied by the bucket filled with the two liters of water.

And beneath the illumination of the neon lights, by the look on the faces of the audience, I realized what they were seeing.

One of them, who had remained seated, stood up, as if out of politeness, and, lifting her skirt out of sync with the others, strangely shifted her weight from foot to foot. Another returned to her seat, groping blindly, her gaze elsewhere. Later, she would order a restorative glass of cognac. Still another kept muttering something, while the man who was the object of all this attention took a cigarette from his breast pocket and lit it with a lighter.

It was a masterful performance.

Like a good impresario, Monsieur Blaise never took his eyes off his audience. One lady, in a tailored suit, walked up to Monsieur Raymond, who didn't move. I cast a glance at Monsieur Blaise, who was visibly worried by this sudden proximity. But there was no cause for concern. The lady was only depositing a bill in the bucket.

"In these cases, it's always a large bill," Monsieur Blaise told us later. "They feel that what they're seeing is worth more than what they paid as an entrance fee. And since they're well off . . . you can imagine, with all those luxury cars at the end of the street waiting for them. It's a little awkward for the bills—once they're wet you have to dry them out. But that's Madame Blaise's job."

"In the beginning," Giraud confided in me, "the Blaises had worried the audience would be overwhelmed, even faint. You never know. But fainting would have meant depriving themselves of this pleasure."

The pleasure bestowed, Monsieur Raymond placed the bucket back down just as he had lifted it up, by folding his knees. Then, with his pants back on, he went to deposit his extinguished cigarette butt in the branded ashtray sitting on the counter. Madame Blaise, who, now that the show was over, had emerged from the kitchen, gave him a fat envelope along with a spiked coffee. In the way he said thank you to Madame Blaise, you could detect the humility of a man who had always worked for a boss. And since he was a man of few words, he shook the hands of her employees, and said, " 'Til Sunday," before heading off onto the streets of Saint-Ouen.

"In the beginning, Raymond was paid by the act," Monsieur Blaise told us, commenting on his exit, "but ever since we started getting a tony audience, he asked to be paid fifty-fifty. It's a better deal for him. But it's fair, basically. He's the one who's dropping his pants. And Madame Blaise doesn't complain because drinks aren't included in the admission price."

I looked around for the woman who had ordered the cognac. Her glass in hand, she was still gazing into the distance and couldn't seem to get over this enchanted Sunday.

"There are three rows of fifteen in the audience," continued Monsieur Blaise. "We can't do more. Especially since I already added chairs. You need them, because some people need to sit down when Raymond pulls out his coat hook. That's why Madame Blaise and I are thinking about a second session. That way, there'd be enough for everyone. We'd like to do Saturdays too, but Raymond prefers Sunday afternoons, so he doesn't have to come back twice."

"Does he live far away?"

"Near Lagny. Not too far, but it's complicated to get here. And he's not alone—he has a wife to keep warm."

"I don't know anyone who can boast of having seen his wife," said Madame Blaise, who had joined the conversation.

"And the lifting of the skirts?"

"That was Monsieur Blaise's idea," continued Madame Blaise. "Raymond said he didn't need all that, but the ladies like it, because each of them can imagine that she's inspiring the feat."

"Does he really need to see all these little panties to exercise his talents?" continued Monsieur Blaise. "Whether they're red, green, or blue, I don't think it matters. It's mostly in his head. No, no, lifting the skirts is just for show. And it flatters the ladies."

"You should have a second career in cabaret," joked Giraud.

"Don't laugh, at one point we thought about adding an accordion."

"That would be a pity. There's a beauty to the silence."

"I was going to say the same thing, Monsieur Giraud. It's like at the circus. Have you ever noticed? Right before the trapeze artists perform their perilous leaps, twenty meters from the ground, everything stops. The music, everything. All you hear is silence. That leaves room for the gasps. One day, in the silence, a lady said, in English: "My God!" I don't know what the good Lord has to do with it. It must have been an American. Now how long it can last, I don't know. It must be like boxing; there must be an age limit. Don't you think?"

Madame Blaise piped in, after a deliberately evasive gesture by Robert Giraud.

"If you ask me, he still has many productive days ahead of him, but in the meantime, his natural gifts ensure his future."

"And then, there's one thing that has to be said, I don't know what you think, but in my opinion Monsieur Raymond provides a service to humanity. Because these ladies," and here Monsieur Blaise lowered his voice, "I'll bet you a drink that not one of them is going to spend her Sunday alone. I always think that being alone, with the image that's in their heads when they leave this place, wouldn't be good for their health."

"Yes, it's a fine service he's providing," concluded Madame Blaise.

The skirts had returned to their usual length as the bistro, little by little, emptied out. Monsieur Blaise, putting the knob back in place, pointed with his chin at those he called the tango dancers who, tipped off to what was going on inside, were pacing at the corner of the Rue Lecuyer.

Returning the way we came, I told Giraud I was surprised to have seen Madame Blaise only once the show was over.

"She never watches. Business doesn't get in the way of modesty. She stays in her kitchen going over the books and only comes out with her envelope when it's over."

· · ·

We separated in front of the Canon d'Or, where Giraud still had some hands to shake. It was too early to go to the Chope des Puces. The musicians only arrived in the afternoon. I took the metro at the Porte de Clignancourt and thought about the adventures that had such an inspirational effect on Giraud. Before we said good-bye, I asked him what to make of the show. His take on it was simple: you couldn't make this stuff up.

15

"A tailor born in Poland has a daughter he's very proud of. She passed her aggregation and teaches French literature. Now that he's retired, the tailor reads a lot. Many books in French, but especially in Yiddish.

"The other day, he asked his daughter: 'Have you read Zola's *L'Assommoir*?'

" 'Yes, of course.'

" 'But have you read it in Yiddish?'

" 'No . . .'

" 'That's too bad! You have to read it in Yiddish!'

"This story shows the pleasure of a mother tongue, wherever you're born."

Ever since I heard Pierre Dumayet tell this story on television, I watch *Lectures pour tous*, the show he hosts with Pierre Desgraupes, whenever I can.

That was how I happened to see the interview Pierre Dumayet conducted with Roger Vailland about his book *A Cold Eye*. A book of essays written between 1945 and 1962. After the conversation, I went to buy the book. "Can one cast a cold eye on everything?"

asked Dumayet. "I think one can cast a cold eye on everything, even on death," said Vailland. "For me, the man with a cold eye is one who has accepted once and for all that life has a beginning and an end, who refuses to fear death, who considers it a natural end to life."

There is only one obstacle, I thought—and I was thinking of this when Vailland announced his plans to devote other essays to this subject—it's when death takes us too early.

I thought about it again, once I had bought and read the book, when already in the forward Vailland reveals his intention to continue the work "at an age when, imagination dried up and the taste for pleasures dulled, I'll have all the time in the world to philosophize."

I had seen this particular show about *L'Assommoir* in Yiddish because it followed a variety show during which Joël Holmès sang. Like Robert, Joël had been a camp counselor at Tarnos. I think that was where he composed his first songs on his guitar. He too had exercised several professions: electrician, salesman, and others. Later, I went to listen to him at the Café de L'Écluse, the cabaret on the Quai des Grands-Augustins. I remember that on the same night were performances by Pia Colombo, Marc and André, and the Limonaire organ of Leo Noel. Later still, at the ABC Music Hall, for several weeks straight, he had been the warm-up to a singing tour by Amália Rodrigues. With a few alums of the summer camp, proud to see Joël's name in bright lights, and proud to know him, we had decided to surprise him after the show by waiting for him at the artists' entrance. We waited in vain. Joël had left his dressing room at the intermission.

My mother was seated next to me during the show when he

sang "Jean-Marie de Pantin." And when she heard: "But there comes one fine night / When 'I love you' are empty words / And it hurts more than you can know / That voice from the past / . . . Yesterday was yesterday / Today is tomorrow / We must love one another / For yesterday, for tomorrow," I saw that she hadn't forgotten her love affairs.

Alex had also started playing the guitar. Not because of Joël, but because of Florencie, to whom I had introduced him. And while until that point he had sworn by Georges Brassens, singing "Celui qui a mal tourné" at the top of his lungs, and had seemed to me uninterested in the music of the past, he started asking who this guy Bruant was, who had written all these songs more than sixty years ago. The very next day he went to Martin Cayla's, a music store on the Faubourg Saint-Martin, to buy a collection of Bruant songs, which he consumed the way one consumes alcohol, without even questioning why they had not disappeared into oblivion. It was under this influence that he in turn began trying to tell stories in music. The minute he got home from school—he was then in tenth grade at the Lycée Voltaire—right after a snack, he went to his room to immerse himself in music. We have never since seen him work with such dedication. Striking and varying the chords, he seemed to be asking his guitar questions, waiting for answers, and he ended up getting them. And this is what I heard through the door one day:

If I say I don't know,
I know more than I show.
The year was forty-two
when he left with his folks.

It was after the first letter from Aunt Esther that Alex had changed his attitude toward school. It had started, naturally, with English. In the hopes of an eventual trip. But then music had followed, soon accompanied by writing.

Although uneven in their results, the texts he wrote at the request of his successive French teachers had already surprised us, and I knew from experience that to attain another truth Alex didn't always worry about veracity. He gave me a work already corrected by his teacher to read, the assignment this time having been to write a story inspired by a newspaper article. He had written five pages in impressive detail about a capital execution based, he told me, on a story he found in a magazine that was lying around our dentist's office, which he had noted at first, then furtively cut out as he was waiting for his appointment. Alex had set the execution before the war, at a time when, as in *Casque d'Or*, guillotine executions took place in public in the early morning on the Boulevard Arago. Through his lawyer, the condemned man Alex wrote about had expressed the wish to drink a café au lait with a fresh and extra crusty buttered baguette on the day of his execution instead of the traditional glass of rum, since he didn't drink alcohol. To the embarrassment of the penitentiary administration, the lawyer had made this known to the press, which immediately seized on the issue. One daily with a wide circulation, finding the subject a juicy one, had even established a poll among its readers in order to see if they thought the condemned's desire should be respected or not. As anticipated, the poll had the effect of increasing circulation the day the results were published. Of the people questioned, 78 percent were resolutely against—some, oddly, out of respect for traditions they deemed sacrosanct; most, however, felt that a person on death row had no right to be making demands and that responding favorably would be shaking the republican order (Alex had put a "sic" after the word "republican"). A great debate ensued, continued Alex. On the airwaves, in the metro as soon as one opened a paper, in the bars, even within families. The intensity of some of these discussions were even reminiscent of those surrounding the Dreyfus affair. Café au lait or glass of rum? The decision of the Ministry of Justice was eagerly anticipated. Government intervention was required. Would the Chamber of Deputies debate the issue? Already, before the date of the execution was even known, the windows of the Boulevard Arago were rented out—for the eventual day—at a king's ransom. Certain pundits, seeking to maintain the interest of a nearly unanimously scandalized population, described in almost poetic language the condemned man sitting in the light of dawn on a wooden stool, a steaming bowl of café au lait between his knees, his trembling, handcuffed hands dunking the buttered bread in the bowl before raising it to his lips. And at that point, as if he had been physically present, in a series of staggering and almost diabolical images, Alex imagined the rest. The crowd wanted to hear the sound of the crusty bread as he chewed, he wrote, but the protestors were making too much noise. Flags were waving, here and there, expressing the anger of those protesting the privileges accorded the assassin while so many deserving families didn't have enough to feed their children. The condemned man, for his part, didn't understand what the ruckus was all about. He didn't understand because his request was not meant to be provocative in any way. He simply wanted, before leaving this world for good, to take with him the memory of one of the rare happy moments he had been given to live.

As an epigraph to his text, Alex had copied the final couplet of a song by Bruant:

And at the guillotine
He paid without a word
Place de la Roquette one fine morning
He showed the folks of Paris
How a pimp knew how to die
from the Bastille square!

Alex's teacher had been shaken by his work, as was I. She had found it remarkable, but, perhaps because it was difficult to believe or rather to accept its authenticity, she had focused on the polling results. The 78 percent, she noted, was very high and made the story less credible. But more important, she highlighted, this exaggerated statistic troubled her, because she wondered why a sixteen-year-old boy would have such a pessimistic vision of the world.

Alex's text brought to mind another story of buttered bread. I was about to file away for future consideration our common need to evoke lives cut short, when a few lines in the news-in-brief section of *France-Soir* caught my eye. A fifty-three-year-old man had committed suicide by eating a camembert laced with arsenic. That was all the paper said. The strangeness of this suicide struck me. How can the two things go together: eating a camembert and choosing to die from it? Choosing both pleasure and death, its opposite? The similarity of this death reminded me of the condemned man's café au lait—the idea that, an instant before dying, he wanted to experience a moment of pleasure. The key difference being that in the second case we were talking about a suicide. And I found it hard to reconcile the contradiction that prompted the suicide victim to end his life by way of a pleasurable experience.

Alex's first buttered bread story dates back several years. Madame Rougemont, for whom my mother worked as a saleslady, had invited her, along with Alex and me, to come for Sunday lunch. "If your mother wants to join us as well, of course, she is most welcome," she had added. But Bubbe didn't want to go. Not only because she wouldn't be comfortable with conversation foreign to her concerns, but because on Sundays, at the Café le Thermomètre, Place de la République, she always met the "Yiddishe-Polnishe-Francouske," with whom she chitchatted about the news of the week.

The "Yiddishe-Polnishe-Francouske" (literally the Jewish-Polish-French woman) owed her nickname to the fact that she was a Jew who had married a Catholic Pole who died on the front in 1939, and then married a Catholic Frenchman, whom she later divorced. All of it, marriages and divorce, in circumstances that remained mysterious to me.

While making excuses for Bubbe's absence, Mother had accepted the invitation for herself and her two sons. So, on the Sunday in question, a bouquet of roses in hand, having instructed Alex on proper behavior, Mother rang the door of Monsieur and Madame Rougemont's apartment, which was located above their store.

The oval table was set for five. Monsieur and Madame Rougemont were at either end, and Mother sat facing Alex and me. Madame Rougemont had prepared a leg of lamb that she had been thoughtful enough to serve with mashed potatoes. Monsieur Rougemont, who, as I learned, was a telecommunications engineer, asked me the inevitable questions one asks an adolescent concerning his studies and professional goals, and since I was expecting those questions and responded appropriately, the meal was proceeding smoothly. It was in the midst of this simple hospitality that Mother gave me a look—not harsh, but firm—suggesting that I should give Alex a kick under the table. He had just built a volcano out of his mashed potatoes. A volcano that was not spewing anything but at the peak of which he had carved out a crater. With his fork, he was already creating another cavity: an underground tunnel into which the lamb juice was meant to flow. Madame Rougemont's mashed potatoes were a perfect consistency and lent themselves to this construction, enabling Alex to avoid the adult conversation. You couldn't fault Alex for his manner of eating mashed potatoes. Even as a baby, Alex was a poor eater, and Leizer had found this trick for getting him to eat. After the airplane accident, Mother, and sometimes I, had taken on that role. When he got older, Alex would tell himself stories, and depending on his mood, using his fork as a tool, the potatoes would become mountains, volcanos, or castles—a certain amount of construction was always needed before they could be consumed.

Monsieur and Madame Rougemont pretended not to notice anything, and Mother's anxiety dissipated when she saw that Alex was coming back to earth and behaving as she had instructed.

Coffee was served in the living room in beautifully decorated English cups. We sat around the coffee table on which, next to a packet of filtered cigarettes which no one touched, sat a box of fancy chocolates which Madame Rougemont circulated as soon as we drank our coffee. It was at that point, when the chocolate was served, that Alex suddenly asked for a piece of bread with butter. Before even glancing over to see Mother's face, I tried to imagine what Madame Rougemont must have thought. Alex had eaten his dinner—lamb, a mountain of mashed potatoes, salad, cheese, a delicious apple tart—and now he was asking for bread and butter to eat with his chocolate. Having no idea how excessive his request might seem, Alex didn't understand why Mother gasped. To the point that when he heard Madame Rougemont, in an effort to be polite, say, "The boy's still hungry," as she headed off to get the bread and butter, he objected, saying that no, he wasn't hungry anymore, but that he was asking for bread to eat with his chocolate. Mother and I knew very well that "the boy" wasn't hungry anymore. It was just that, since nursery school, Alex had always had a buttered baguette with a bar of chocolate as an after-school snack. And since he enjoyed them together, he saw no reason to deprive himself of that pleasure. It was to better enjoy this wonderful chocolate that he wanted to savor it together with a buttered baguette.

Here again, habit had won out. He couldn't help himself.

And it was while Madame Rougemont was politely offering Alex a second chocolate to accompany his remaining bread, so that this innocent pleasure could be prolonged, that Monsieur Rougemont launched into a story that had absolutely nothing to do with what we had been discussing.

It is important that I remember this story because of the way it turned out. To the extent that I remember it correctly, it had happened to him when he was around twenty years old. He had decided, with some young people his age, to go on a hike in the mountains. They walked for several hours before reaching the peak. It was a glacier, if I recall correctly. Being competitive by nature, in fact, Monsieur Rougemont was the one to reach the peak first. And with enough advance on the others, he'd had time to undress—it was summer and it was hot—and jump into a lake right at his feet, just steps away. "And that's when I had the scare of my life," Monsieur Rougemont told us, "because the surface of the water was ten meters below me. Ten meters! That's a long way! The time to reach the water was so incomprehensible that I thought there was no water, and that I had been the victim of an optical illusion. When I resurfaced and saw my friends applauding my audacity—they themselves had measured the distance to the water correctly—I realized what had happened. It's an optical phenomenon that's common in the mountains due to the refraction of the solar rays. It's a kind of mirage. In a desert, it produces the illusion of a pool of water. In the mountains, on the snow or in the ice, it eliminates distances."

Monsieur Rougemont had told this story simply to change the topic. And yet, when he got to this point in the story, thinking back, he was practically shaking. He concluded by saying, "It's a feeling that's difficult to explain. I don't even think you can really understand it unless you've had this kind of experience firsthand."

To everyone's surprise, Alex chimed in. "The same thing happened to me. One day, the lights were out in the hallway. Since I thought there was only one step left, I jumped. But there were two. I was really afraid too."

I had seen faces lose their composure before. I think I've even seen them change color: white, or tending toward green, sometimes

purple. But from what I remember years later of Monsieur Rougemont's face it was all those colors at once. Here was this jerky little
kid, a nine-year-old punk, daring to compare his heroic story—
which he had no doubt told dozens of time to great effect—to the
petty story of a missed step.

Did Alex have the slightest idea of what he was doing to Monsieur Rougemont? His comment had such destructive power that
this man, who had been nice enough to invite us to lunch, lost all
capacity to respond. He seemed devastated. That was Alex's talent. To evoke such a reaction while preserving an appearance of
innocence. It was high art.

With the offenses accumulating and the hole at risk of getting deeper, Mother decided it was time to head back to the Rue
Oberkampf, and she didn't wait to get home to tell Alex that she
would never take him anywhere ever again. And since she felt
like walking, we returned home on foot. Alex followed ten steps
behind, walking on the edge of the sidewalk, hands deep in his
pockets, eyes on the gutter, like a bum looking for a cigarette butt.

16

It was after attending a class given by philosopher and resistance fighter Vladimir Jankélévitch at the Sorbonne that I went to the Studio des Ursulines to see *The Earrings of Madame de . . .* by Max Ophuls. And after another one of his classes, on time, I obtained the text of *Reigen*, the play by Arthur Schnitzler that Max Ophuls adapted to make the film *La Ronde*.

Schnitzler's play began like this:

I
The Girl and the Soldier

At night, near the public park, on the banks of the Danube.

THE SOLDIER appears, whistling. He is on his way back to the barracks.

THE GIRL: How about it, handsome?

THE SOLDIER turns and continues on his way.

THE GIRL: Want to come with me?

THE SOLDIER: You calling me handsome?

The beginning as filmed by Max Ophuls didn't exist in the play. The beginning of the film is the one in which a character comes out of the fog and addresses the audience as he walks, asking, "What part do I play in this story? The author? . . ."

Ophuls's memoirs, written during his exile in Hollywood, had just been published. He told of his hasty departure from Germany in February 1933. "If your father is sick," they had advised him by phone, "don't waste another day, take the train immediately." Ophuls had understood. "That night, as we were heading toward the Zoo train station," he wrote, "I drove past the Atrium, one of Berlin's main theaters. Splashed across the facade, big illuminated letters announced: LIEBELEI, A FILM BY MAX OPHULS. I turned toward my wife and son and told them, 'Look carefully, it's probably the last time you'll see this.' "

What Arthur Schnitzler, who died in 1931, couldn't know, Max Ophuls did know when he filmed La Ronde in 1950. Hence, in my view, the introduction of the "master of ceremonies" character, Max Ophuls's double, saying in Vienna, in 1900, that "the past is so much more certain than the future."

When I saw La Ronde for the first time, this observation about the past and the future puzzled me. Only now do I feel I can fathom its true meaning.

I owe this revelation to Vladimir Jankélévitch, and to my good fortune at having attended his class on Time. To this little phrase which I remembered: "Time in the past is always good."

These two men, Ophuls and Jankélévitch, were both born at the turn of the century. As if there were some natural connection, I sensed that I would now vacillate from one to the other. It was therefore fitting to see *The Earrings of Madame de* . . . upon leaving Jankélévitch's class.

A seemingly frivolous woman learns to love again and it kills her—that's the story of the film.

On the big screen, Danielle Darrieux, her forehead pressed against a closing door, tries to defend herself against love, telling the man she loves: "I don't love you, I don't love you, I don't love you." In the audience, seated near me, a young woman was watching intently and crying. Her tears, brought on by these "I don't love yous," seemed to reflect a painful memory which she may have thought forgotten. Falling in with those of the film's heroine, they slid silently, like restorative tears. Perhaps because this woman near me was crying the way one cries from experience, I don't think I've ever had a better screening of a love story. And I wondered why the beautiful love stories that I adored in film (*Casque d'Or, Jules et Jim, The Earrings of Madame de* . . .), despite their charm, always ended tragically with death seen in the gaze of those who remain.

After the screening, I took a few steps in the direction of the Rue Gay-Lussac and waited for the young woman with whom I had just seen *The Earrings of Madame de* . . . Yes, with. Even though I didn't know her. With, because we were so close to one another watching Danielle Darrieux and Vittorio De Sica together, living on love and dying of it. I didn't know what I was going to say to her, but I waited for her. And since I was waiting for her, she stopped near me. And since I didn't know her, I excused myself and told her that during the film, when she cried, I had wanted to take her hand in mine and hold it there, and I again excused myself for what I had just said. She said thank you. And this thank you was said in a way I didn't know it could be said. And we were silent. And then, she made a slight gesture. Her right hand slowly lifted from her body, stopped halfway, and gently returned to her side. But this start of a gesture wasn't aborted, since I had no difficulty continuing it and experiencing her touch in my mind.

Her face still bore the traces of her tears when she crossed the Rue des Ursulines. On the sidewalk, at the corner of the Rue Gay-Lussac, she stopped for a brief instant. Was she waiting for me? I don't think so. She turned around. What separated us? I don't know. I stood watching her disappear.

There had been only those words: thank you, and a gesture that stayed with me, and that lasted long enough to know that anything had been possible.

Vladimir Jankélévitch's class, which I had attended that very morning, was a class on the moment. The opportunity of the moment. And as I watched the young woman disappear, some fragments of Jankélévitch's words came to mind which I had barely had time to jot down: "It's the enchanted moment, when gaze meets gaze"; "It's the instant that is brief and therefore precious"; "Our life is made of unique instants"; "It's perhaps my life's meaning that is passing in a flash"; "How can I capture this fleeting moment?"

I would long remember this moment I had been unable to capture. And perhaps simply because I was attached to the ephemeral, I hadn't sought to hold onto it.

I decided to walk a bit. And only at the Hôtel de Ville did I take bus number 96 to return home.

The class by Vladimir Jankélévitch reminded me of another

precious moment, which also could only take place once since it was a first. I don't know how old I was. Thirteen or fourteen, maybe, but barely. After the summer camp, several of us decided to go swimming once a week so that we wouldn't lose track of one another. We chose the Neptuna pool, on the Grands Boulevards, which was closest to our respective homes. This pool with its overhanging dressing rooms was unique in that the dressing rooms were separated by just a thin wooden divider. By chance, one time Suzy was in the dressing room next to mine. And I had barely taken off my swimsuit—it was after swimming—when I heard Suzy wringing hers out. And then I heard the sound of rubbing. The towel against her body? I listened to the movement of her arms, almost trembling. It was then, drying myself with the same gesture as she used, that I saw a hole pierced in the divider less than a meter from the ground. It was small, for sure, but apparently drilled for an eye to peep through. Which mine did—something I remember doing with little hesitation. There, so close, a few centimeters away, was Suzy's naked body. She was conscientiously drying each part of her body right before my eyes, and I discovered, filled with wonder, what the movements of her towel allowed me to see. Then, as if to better offer a view of her body, she dried her hair thoroughly before sitting down, opposite me, on the little white bench that was in every changing room. She dried one leg then the other, successively, and strangely, as if her mind were wandering, she sat there, waiting, hands on her knees in an state of immobility that was all that I could ask for. And then, almost obediently, as if responding to my request, slowly she let her knees fall apart. And what appeared before me was dazzling. Close to fainting, I saw where all my longing was leading me. And

I had no other desire at that time than just to look. I didn't yet imagine anything else. Since then I have had occasion to see other nude bodies, but because of this memory, which I still like to linger over, this passion for nudity has never left me, and it is always in broad daylight that I like to perform the acts of love.

This moment when Suzy was showing me all the treasure of her body ended abruptly. She in turn had noticed the hole in our dividing wall—even though, upon reflection, perhaps she had been aware of it for some time. Her curiosity equaled my own. She knelt down, approaching her face to mine. I was up in a flash. What should I do? Even though I was already dry, I pretended to towel myself off, and that was it. Our bodies were saying the same things, to the point that when we left our cabins, glancing at one another, I said to myself: how similar we are. And we never ever spoke about what had happened, of what we had just shared.

Outside on the sidewalk of the Boulevard Poissonière, the others were waiting for us. Speaking as usual of this and that, we walked to the Place de la République, where we separated. Suzy and I each went our own way. In the beach bag hanging from her shoulder was the towel, still damp from her body, the beauty of which she had allowed me to contemplate moments earlier.

17

A sweet spring-like sun flooded the terrace, and yet Ruth had decided to sit and wait for me in the back of the Café le Centenaire, where we had agreed to meet. She had phoned that morning, fairly early, to say that she was in Paris for a few days.

I had met Ruth the previous summer at the Bonnat Museum in Bayonne. It was during one of my days off from the summer camp at Tarnos. I wasn't familiar with Léon Bonnat, one of the most famous painters of the Third Republic, to whom the city of Bayonne, his birthplace, had devoted an entire museum. It was very warm that day and I figured it would be cooler spending the afternoon in this museum than watching a game of Basque pelota with Guy, another counselor. Although I was struck by Bonnat's impressive technical mastery, I couldn't help feeling bored with the work, which seemed so representative of bourgeois academism that I ended up passing very quickly by an entire series of official portraits. Thanks to which I noticed a young girl in sandals and a ponytail whose body language seemed to express the same reservations. It was Ruth. She had seen me smile at the face she had made at a painting and that was how we met. And since it had seemed silly to shake hands and say good-bye right after leaving the museum, we had gone to sit at a little bistro under the arcade of the Rue du Pont-Neuf.

"What do you do? Are you on vacation?" Ruth had asked after telling me that she was a German history student.

I told her about the summer camp where, first as a camper, and now as a counselor, I had been coming for several years. Probably because of what I told her about the origins of the camp, and without seeking to find out more, as if that were enough for her, Ruth almost blurted out that she had come to see the internment camp in Gurs, but that she was staying in Bayonne because there was a youth hostel there.

"You don't know . . . yes, you must know the camp at Gurs," she had said, seeing how surprised I was.

"Yes, I've heard about it; I know it was one of the camps in the south of France during the war, but I didn't know it was near Bayonne. But I'm surprised that you know about it. How do you know about this camp? And why do you want to visit it?"

"My history professor told me about it. He was interned there. He fled Germany under Hitler before the war and like many anti-fascists he came to France. But here, since he was German, he was interned starting in 1939 at Gurs, where there were already fighters from the war in Spain. And that's why I wanted to see what it was like."

"Do they teach the history of French camps in German universities?"

"No, no, not at all. Never. It was outside of class that my professor told me about it."

Ruth, whose command of French was quite good, told me that

she had broken off all relations with her father when he had refused to answer any of her questions regarding his activities while he wore the Wehrmacht uniform, arguing that children had no right to judge their fathers. She had begun to question her father after reading an article that appeared in a sociological review. The article, ironically entitled "Memoirs of a Parisian Occupation," was written by an architect who, at the beginning of 1944, at the age of seventeen, had enlisted in the German army. Ruth left her house, declaring—somewhat histrionically, she admitted—that she would never set foot in the house again until her father told her how he had won all his medals. Breaking her isolation, she had opened up to her history professor, which is how she ended up in France.

"What I hated most of all was being kept in the dark," added Ruth. Because of that, I can only imagine the worst. That's what my parents don't understand."

"And do you think one day you'll reconnect with your father?"

"I don't know. I don't think so. Obedience is sacred to him. Since he himself was brought up in a very authoritarian fashion, he can't accept losing that. Especially with a daughter. That's why I don't have much hope in that regard."

"So how do you live?"

"My mother gives me some money behind my father's back, and aside from that, I'm a model."

"A model . . . for magazines?"

"No, not for magazines, I'm not thin enough for that. I'm a model at a painting academy."

"So you pose . . ."

"Nude, yes. If that's what you're asking."

I was silent a moment, unable to stop myself from trying to imagine Ruth naked, then represented on multiple canvasses or drawing papers. And I liked what had brought her here.

"Do you know Franz Hessel?"

"Do *you* know Franz Hessel?"

Ruth was so surprised to hear me say the name Franz Hessel, who, according to her, even in Germany, was almost unknown, that she answered my question with the same question. So I told her about *Jules and Jim*. My two days on the set. The three kisses with Laura cut in the editing process, but leaving out the importance these three kisses held for me. I told her about Chez Victor. The bistro table at which Oskar Werner had drawn the portrait of Lucie. Jeanne Moreau. The missed appointment. And Ruth told me, "I'll be back, Bernard, and you'll show me the Paris of *Jules and Jim*."

So Ruth had returned to Paris and was waiting for me in the back of Café le Centenaire. Because bus number 96 passed right in front on its way to Belleville, I thought it was a good place to start our journey.

Her arrival in Paris had been preceded by a postcard showing the Berlin Zoo, on the back of which she had written:

Franz Hessel: Born in Stettin (the German name for Szczecin) in 1880.

Arrived in Berlin in 1888.

Met Henri Pierre Roché in Paris in 1906.

In 1913, married Helen Grund, whom he'd met in Paris in 1912.

Translator of Stendhal, Baudelaire, and Proust.

In 1920, his novel *Pariser Romanze* appeared.

In 1931, he composed a portrait of Marlene Dietrich.

In 1940, interned in the Milles camp, in the south of France.

Released after several months.

He died on January 6, 1941, in Sanary-sur-Mer.

And Ruth sent me kisses.

On the bus, which took us to Ménilmontant from the Rue Oberkampf, Ruth specified the reason for her visit to France. She was increasingly interested in the history of art, and since, as she said, she was marked for life by what she was gradually learning about the histories of the camps, she had decided to go visit the camp at Milles. In researching Franz Hessel for me, she learned that, fleeing the Nazi regime, Max Ernst, Hans Hartung, Hans Bellmer, Max Lingner, and dozens of other German and Austrian painters had been interned at this camp at the beginning of the war. She had heard that some of their works, and in particular some large murals by Lingner, were still there. She was happy and moved to tears to be starting her visit of Paris on the bus. As soon as she stepped on the deck, she thought of a drawing by Lingner. It was a picture of a bus, identical in every way to the one we were on. It was the 85 instead of the 96. What had amused her about the drawing was the inclusion of a bicyclist wearing short pants and a cap who was smiling at the passengers while holding the rail of the bus's deck, and moving without pedaling.

Max Lingner had lived a long time in Paris.

To walk to all these promised sites, I had suggested getting off at the Julien-Lacroix stop, right in front of the photographer of the Rue de Ménilmontant. From there, without stopping in front of the building where my father had worked, I followed quite naturally and effortlessly the memory of my meeting with Robert. And covering this territory with Ruth brought back memories which, I now knew, would never entirely leave me.

On the Rue Vilin, in front of Madame Rayda's shutter, with its promises of joy and heartbreak, Ruth took my picture. She insisted.

Chez Nadine was closed. I was sorry about this especially because of the painting that Anatole Jakowsky had shown us, which would have really interested Ruth.

She took other pictures: of the ocher-colored bakery on the Rue des Envierges, the Villa Castel, the Villa Ottoz, the workshop of the *Casque d'Or*, the pedestrian overpass on the Rue de la Mare, and of a commemorative plaque on the railing of the Rue de Ménilmontant, above the little belt railway train tracks:

FRANÇOIS BOLTZ, 38 YEARS OF AGE

GODEFROY LOUIS, 53 YEARS OF AGE

ADJEMAN, 50 YEARS OF AGE

AND TWO UNKNOWN PATRIOTS

DIED 23 AUGUST 1944

FOLLOWING A VICTORIOUS ATTACK ON NAZI TRAINS.

Next we took the Rue de Savies, dotted with its medieval boundary markers, at the top of which we reached the manhole on the Rue des Cascades. And finally, on the other side of the Place des Fêtes, behind the gate at the back of the Impasse Compans, the bucolic space where Chez Victor is located. Charmed, Ruth took a picture of the little stage, and from the stage a photo to the east of Paris. The bocce players were there, but she didn't have the nerve to photograph them. The man with the white hair was there too, at the same table, and closed his newspaper when he saw us arrive. I introduced them. Monsieur Victor approached, and I introduced him as well: "Monsieur Victor, the owner of this place, Ruth, a friend." She ordered a hot chocolate, as did I, but with more milk.

Ever since the reading of the Victor Hugo poem and the singing of "Le Temps des Cerises," I was a regular at Chez Victor.

I had learned a lot from the man with the white hair.

"I come to this bistro in part because it's one of the last places in Paris where you can wake to the rooster's crow," he had told me the day of our first conversation.

"Do you sleep here sometimes?"

"No, I sleep at home, and I've never been here early enough to hear it. But just knowing it brings me here."

I took advantage of my visit with Ruth to return the copy of Hippolyte Prosper Olivier Lissagaray's *History of the Commune of 1871* that he'd lent me. I had protected it by covering it with clear paper; it was a rare edition that was almost impossible to find, published by the Librairie du Travail in 1929. As he flipped through it mechanically, a handwritten piece of paper fell out that I must have slipped into the flyleaf and forgotten to remove. "This must be yours," he said, handing it to me without reading it.

We didn't speak about the book, putting that off to a later date. Because she was German, he was curious about Ruth's curiosity. As we were leaving, she asked if she could photograph him, and he acquiesced with a smile.

"In '14, I was wounded on one of the first days of the war," he said, as soon as he heard the click, "and in '40 I was too old to fight.

And now I'll be going to Germany in a photo. That's good. A more peaceful way to go."

And when Ruth asked him where she could send the photo, he said:

"Send it to Bernard, he knows where to find me. Right here, except on Sundays."

"What did Bernard tell you about me?" he said to Ruth, after they were introduced. "He must have mentioned that I'm someone who lives in the past. We talk a lot about the past together, even though we're talking about different pasts. Because of the differences in our ages, of course, but not only. People don't experience events in the same way. He may have told you that, even though he doesn't like to talk about it much. What amazes me is that he likes the same songs as I do. Generally it's the music that distinguishes generations, but he knows the songs by Aristide Bruant by heart, for example, even though Bruant had been dead fifteen years when Bernard was born. I also like Bruant a lot, but my favorite song is "The Red Mound" by Montéhus. It's from the twenties. Listen, the refrain goes like this:

They call it the Red Mound
Baptized it was one morning
When every one of those who climbed
Rolled into the gully.

Today it is full of vines
Where the grapes are growing
And whosoever drinks this wine
Drinks the blood of his buddies.

I couldn't get over it. It was the first time I was hearing the man with the white hair sing. The man who could listen for hours without talking. Even Monsieur Victor stopped serving to listen.

"The Butte Rouge isn't near here, it's on the other side of Paris. But it could have been here, in Belleville, because Belleville has seen a lot of bloodshed from those who came from every corner of Europe. 'Belleville will save Europe,' an orator said at the time of the Commune. It was naive and not very realistic, but you can also think of it another way. That people leaving Italy, Poland, Armenia, or Russia, who came to France with their families, were welcomed in Belleville."

And the man with the white hair wouldn't stop. This time, he spoke about the Paris Commune. The final battles on the Rue Ramponneau. The taking of Père-Lachaise. Of the Communards' Wall. But also about the time when, to shake off the week's fatigue, he would come here with his wife to dance to the accordion or tango when Chez Victor was a Saturday night dance hall. "Do you know how to dance the tango?"

Oh! how I loved the ladies
And how they loved me! . . . I was such a looker!
Need to go back in reverse
The way you dance the tango!

"That's by Caussimon. Jean-Roger Caussimon. A poet. Poetry is always beautiful. One day I realized that I owed everything to poetry. Because you can say everything with poetry. You just need to make time for it. Knowing the French language as well as you know it, Mademoiselle, that too is a beautiful thing. And that's why you need to come back, because languages change over time. It's good to learn a language by studying it, but you also have to live it. A living language is noisier, and the street is a good place to hear it. For example, if I could go backward like you, I'd have twenty springtimes behind me. But I can't. Instead I've had three times as many, I'm a sixty-year-old. Meanwhile, if someone told me I've lived through sixty springtimes, I would say it was a mistake, because over time, the years change in nature. One day, perhaps, I'll have had eighty go-rounds. Anyway, I hope to make it that far. Especially for my grandson. So that he'll remember he had a grandfather. You see, we've talked a lot about the past, because of nostalgia. Nostalgia is good because it makes things present that no longer are. But it's my grandson, in fact, who taught me to love the present. Because every day he does something he didn't do the day before and which he may not do again the next day. When he started crawling, he moved as fast as I walk. Now he walks, he never crawls, as if he didn't remember how anymore. So I'm happy I enjoyed it while it lasted. It's the same with talking. He likes yogurt. He calls it 'nanouth.' But we don't correct him because one day he'll say 'yogurt' just like everyone else."

"How old is your grandson?"

"He just turned twenty-one months."

Stirred up by memories that were not her own, Ruth climbed onto the stage as we exited. Before her, a Paris so rich in humanity, too vast to possess, seemed to reverberate with all that she had just heard.

"What's that man's name?"

"I don't know. When I asked Monsieur Victor, he told me: 'His first name is Jules, like Vallès.'"

"Vallès? Who is Vallès?

"Vallès . . . was a journalist and writer. But not the kind that Henri Pierre Roché's characters Jules or Jim would have known. This Jules was always a rabble-rouser. He founded a newspaper, *The Cry of the People*, and he was named a member of the Paris Commune. After their victory, the Versaillais condemned him to death, but he took refuge in England and came back to France only after the amnesty of 1880. I just started reading a trilogy he wrote which was published posthumously."

"That's three Jules then," said Ruth, laughing. "The one we just saw, what did he used to do?"

"He worked in shoes, like a lot of the people who live in this neighborhood. In fact, most of those who live in the eleventh, twentieth, and nineteenth arrondissements are small artisans. In the book I just returned to him, I read that they had counted almost three thousand communards working in the wood industry."

After each response, Ruth felt the need to know more; when she sensed that there was something that couldn't quite be said, she would precede her question with a silence which she tried to bridge by glancing around.

"Can you tell me what was on that paper that was in the book?" she asked, looking at her feet. "Unless it's too personal . . ." and she looked up at me.

"No, it's not personal. Well, let's just say that it was for personal reasons, but I can tell you because it's something I copied from the book."

I took out the paper, which I had folded and placed in my pocket, and as I continued to walk, I read slowly:

"The Versaillais are slitting throats in Paris and Paris is

oblivious to it. The night is blue, starry, warm, laden with the scent of spring. The theaters are crowded. The boulevards are bustling with life."

I had copied this text from Lissagaray because when I read it I had wondered what my beloved Paris had been doing on the morning of July 16, 1942, when more than thirteen thousand Jewish men, women, and children were rounded up and taken to the Vélodrome d'Hiver, as if history were repeating itself. And I kept wondering if this "obliviousness" wasn't an echo of the one that Lissagaray had described almost a century earlier. Maybe I'm exaggerating, but maybe that is also why I feel stricken each time the Paris Commune is mentioned.

I said a few words about this to Ruth. After, there were still some hesitant questions. Some, no doubt, were left unspoken, while others were not:

"And the 'Communards' Wall' that Monsieur Jules spoke about, what is that?"

"That's the wall where the Versaillais shot the last defenders of the Commune. It's in the Père-Lachaise cemetery. Each year, at the end of the month of May, a procession still passes by it to commemorate the event."

When we reached the Boulevard de Belleville the streetlights came on, projecting their glow onto the still naked trees. In the past, before I became a regular at Chez Victor, this simultaneity would have reinforced my feeling that I was entering into real Parisian territory.

The previous summer, Ruth had told me: "I'll be back, Bernard, and you'll show me the Paris of *Jules and Jim*." Now here she was, and I realized, descending the Rue Oberkampf, that the Paris we were seeing wasn't the Paris promised but the one shown in Truffaut's film. The other Paris, the one in the novel, was more in the zone of Montparnasse, a place where I am not connected by any memories.

Anyway, what would we have seen at Le Dôme or La Coupole? Whom would we have met? I was worried that Ruth might be feeling disappointed, and thought I should explain this when, more impressed than I would have imagined by what she had seen and heard, she asked if it would be possible to see this "Communards' Wall" that Monsieur Jules, the man with the white hair, had spoke about so emotionally.

So the next day—a Sunday—we met at the Père-Lachaise cemetery, at the so-called "Porte des Amandiers," because it was the one closest to the metro station. But since the Communards' Wall was diagonally across the cemetery, we still had a long hike to get there.

I visit cemeteries on occasion, even when there is no burial or demonstration. I don't know why. Even now, with Ruth, I wasn't too sure what we were accomplishing. She hadn't brought her camera. Was it out of respect? At first she regretted it, then she forgot about it. Her regret was prompted by the tombstones, or rather by the names engraved on them, which she hadn't been expecting. Amid the inextricable tangle of unknown tombs, so many famous names! Famous painters! Corot, Daumier, Delacroix, Géricault, Ingres, Pissarro, Modigliani. Modigliani, whom Roché and Hessel had probably known during his lifetime. And, as if it were all preordained, as we turned our backs on Seurat's tomb, we found that of Vallès. One of the three Juleses. The rebel was represented here by a sculpted bust, with a beard and mustache.

And then, another coincidence. Or chance? Or what? As she gazed at the tomb of Frederic Chopin, Ruth didn't see me jump. Right nearby, in front of me, these words were engraved:

HERE RESTS GINETTE NEVEU AND HER BROTHER JEAN

VICTIM OF THE AERIAL CATASTROPHE OVER THE AZORES

OCTOBER 28, 1949

Here rests? First, why the singular for "rests" and "victim" when there are two of them? Once the name is written in stone, isn't one dead person worth another? And most of all, if these two are resting here, in Père-Lachaise, where is Leizer, where is Alex's father, who was on the same plane?

But I had no time to recover from this coincidence. Ruth was calling me: "Which way is it?" drawing me away from these victims, or what remained of them.

It was further along. Ten minutes more and we were there. A long stone wall and a simple plaque: TO THOSE WHO SACRIFICED FOR THE COMMUNE, MAY 21–28, 1871.

"How many people were shot here?" asked Ruth.

"I don't know exactly. But they say that during what they call 'The Bloody Week' 20,000 people were killed."

I remembered that behind us, facing the wall, there was the tomb of Jean-Baptiste Clément, which I absolutely wanted to show Ruth because of the resemblance to Monsieur Jules. He was the author not only of "Le Temps des Cerises," but also of "La Semaine Sanglante," a song dedicated to those shot during the Bloody Week of 1871.

But Ruth didn't seem to be listening to me anymore. She was

looking not at Clément but behind him, on the other side of what is called the Avenue Circulaire—because although it is barely larger than a path, this so-called avenue rings the Père-Lachaise cemetery almost in its entirety. Behind the Communards' Wall— and this I hadn't thought about the day before, when Ruth had asked me to see the Wall—behind the Communards' Wall are monuments. Four monuments dedicated to the memory of those deported to the concentration and extermination camps. Auschwitz-Birkenau. Ravensbrück. Neuengamme. Mauthausen.

Ruth was discovering that the Communards' Wall and these four monuments faced one another. And there, without moving, she took my hand. For whom? For herself? For me? She was facing something that, in her country, the country of her birth, the country in which she grew up, was nameless, wasn't taught in school. So because it was all she could do, she took my hand. I knew that she wasn't looking at me and though I didn't look at her either, my hand was also holding hers. We took a few steps without letting go, saying nothing. What more could you say than what these monuments, on which no names were engraved, were already saying? A patch of ground in a Parisian cemetery below which no bodies were resting. These monuments were here so that we should remember, and perhaps, though I wasn't thinking this at the time, Ruth had just realized why she had come.

We continued on our path in silence, trying in vain to think about something else. We had an opportunity with a group of tourists who were putting flowers on a grave to our left. Curiosity, adding to our desire to be distracted from our thoughts, propelled us to investigate what was happening. It was the tomb of Marcel

Proust, to whom these Japanese, passing through Paris, were paying homage.

One of them who spoke French explained to us that it was a duty and an honor for them to place flowers on the tomb of a writer who was a veritable cult figure. He was brusquely interrupted by a female voice exclaiming her indignation:

"I'm sick of Proust! I'm sick of Proust!"

Dressed in a long dark coat with a hood, the woman who was yelling was walking with large steps in a parallel alley, looking only at the spot on the ground where she was stepping.

"She comes every morning," explained a groundskeeper from whom we later gathered information. Her son brings her here before going to work, and another family member picks her up at lunchtime. In between she walks from end to end through the rows, giving bread to the birds and kicking the cats."

"But why does she hate Proust?"

"It's not especially Proust. One day it's Proust, another it's Balzac, another Sarah Bernhardt, any time there's a crowd around the grave of someone famous. That's all we know. But she never gets any more violent than this, so we don't pay attention to her anymore."

"But why does her son bring her to the cemetery? Wouldn't she be better off in a park, like the Buttes-Chaumont?"

"That's what we thought in the beginning. We even spoke to the family about it. But she's the one who wants to come here, it seems. Probably she knows more people here among the dead than among the living at the Buttes-Chaumont. Anyway, that's what we groundskeepers figure is the story."

• • •

We went to the Chope des Puces to eat fries and listen to gypsy jazz. It was a good choice for Ruth, who liked both. It was good because we took the 85 bus, the one Max Lingner had drawn, to get there. Leaning on the rail of the rear deck of the bus, Ruth watched the flow of pedestrians on the sidewalks of the Boulevard Barbès and the Boulevard Ornano as they headed to the Porte de Clignancourt.

After the fries and the gypsy guitarists, we endeavored to head up the Rue Paul-Bert, where on makeshift shelves awaited trinkets which in their day had no doubt been precious to someone. By trying to take in everything in her line of sight, Ruth saw nothing. I was looking for a souvenir to give her. It was tough because I had no idea what it might be. It was chance, which I don't much believe in since the eye sees what it seeks, that this time came through. On an American army cot sat a little yellow hardcover book. On the cover was a picture of a man with a mustache, the kind you meet at Monsieur Victor's. It was a photo book by Robert Doisneau. I opened it and read the following: "The texts on pages 21–24, 43–48, 59–66, and 111–122 are by Robert Giraud." I bought it instantly. And while flipping through it, I went to join Ruth, who was bent over a series of old penholders, and asked her to listen as I read:

"The true attraction of the bistro, meaning the neighborhood bistro, is something else for the regular. An hour to kill after work, before heading home, spent with friends who always gather at the same place, around the same counter, the same table. Everyone knows one another, everyone speaks as familiars with one another, everyone is at home."

I closed the book and gave it to Ruth. And quite naturally, we switched to the more informal "tu."

• • •

That evening, after Ruth went to get her backpack and camera at the hotel, we met at the Gare de Lyon. We said good-bye on the platform and, whereas the idea of going to Germany had never crossed my mind, she invited me to come spend a few days in Berlin.

"A few days in Berlin? But why?"

"You don't need a why. For me."

With that, she planted a quick kiss on my lips and jumped on the train.

Several weeks after Ruth's departure I decided to go see the camp at Drancy, the internment camp from which the convoys had departed for Auschwitz.

Although the two days we spent together must have played a role in this decision, it wasn't because of them. There is no lack of reasons to go to Drancy.

What was left to see? As in the well-known photographs, the buildings formed a U-shape with a large space where the round-ups must have taken place in the center. These buildings were now inhabited. There were even curtains on the windows.

Where to begin?

I was drawn to a few people who from a distance didn't seem to be residents. I approached. A photographer was directing a fifty-year-old man leaning on a column. With his camera around his neck, the photographer was trying to place the man's head, holding it by the chin and explaining that it was better for the light.

"Don't touch me!" cried the man suddenly. "Don't touch me. If you want to take pictures, take pictures! But don't touch me! You want to be a director? Go be a director. But not with me! I'm not an actor. I go where I want, and where I can. That's all!"

"But I take pictures people ask me to take. And people ask me to take what they want."

"Because you think you know what people want? Do people even know what they want? You're a photographer? So take the pictures you want to take. You! Just you! Now you want to get into people's heads? What people? I don't know people. Listen to me: I'm going to keep going where I want, and if I want to go nowhere, I'll go nowhere, and you'll have to deal with that! But do not, do not touch me!"

I walked away.

Another group arrived. A woman surrounded by teenagers. She was telling them that many children who were less than four years old and were transferred there from the camps at Pithiviers and Beaune-la-Rolande didn't know their names. I remembered that, as soon as Alex knew how to say a few words, my mother kept telling him: "Repeat after me: my name is Alex Zygelman, my name is Alex Zygelman." It seems that I too learned to say my name very young: Bernard Appelbaum.

18

I lied to my mother. I didn't tell her I was going to Berlin. Based on the tone of her voice when she asked me one day if I had had any news from "my" German, I knew what she'd think of the plan.

She had seen me reading the letters Flaubert wrote in Croisset to Louise Colet and I had come up with the idea of telling her that I could better savor these letters if I spent a few days in Rouen, where Flaubert had written most of his work. This wasn't entirely a lie, since I was curious to take that trip. I knew that, aside from the garden pavilion by the water, nothing remained, that his house had been destroyed, but in any case this place was still synonymous with Flaubert and might teach me something about his letters.

As with the Roger Vailland book, I read this correspondence thanks to a Pierre Dumayet television program devoted to Gustave Flaubert.

"When we think of a friend, we remember his voice," Dumayet had said. "And for those who love his works, Gustave Flaubert is like a friend. Of course, we don't know what his voice sounded like. But in the letters he wrote, you can detect his speaking style, his spontaneity."

I thought of Ruth often. I remembered her voice, I really wanted to go see her. Nonetheless several months passed before I decided to accept to her invitation. Not only to avoid hurting my mother, who wouldn't have understood my going to a country where they speak only German, and to whom I would simply have to tell a story about where I was going, but because I knew it would be hard for me, on the streets of Berlin, not to imagine every man I met over the age of forty-five—no doubt many of them—dressed in a Wehrmacht uniform.

I knew my mother would understand, but I preferred to lie than leave her heavy-hearted.

So, Berlin.

Ruth was waiting for me at the train station, smiling, standing back slightly. I figured that this train station, right near the zoo, must have been the one through which the Ophuls family, and many others, had passed in order to flee Nazi Germany.

Ruth's smile was reassuring. It consoled me after the presence in my compartment of two men in Tyrolean lederhosen. They'd gotten on the train at some point—I must have been sleeping—and I couldn't understand a word they said, despite my knowledge of Yiddish, which generally was very helpful.

Ruth didn't live far from the station. Ten minutes' walk on the Knesebeckstrasse, not far from the Kurfürstendamm, where we went for a cup of coffee with Chantilly cream, accompanied by a cake that was impressive in its height, at least double what you'd find in a Parisian patisserie.

Once we got to her apartment—a small studio that belonged to a friend of her mother's, on the top floor of a rather fancy building—and I put down my suitcase, she gave me the choice of resting or going for a walk. To the zoo, perhaps, which in her opinion was worth seeing. She had an important meeting that would last about two hours and which she had been unable to cancel. I opted for the walk. She accompanied me to the zoo, and since I had only French money in my pocket, she gave me a few marks, just in case.

I passed rapidly by the birds of prey, which held no attraction for me, and hurried past the reptile building—I have never understood the fascination for these creatures by those unusual collectors who enjoy wearing them wrapped around their necks like scarves when they get home from work. Instead I looked for the monkeys, enclosed in their tall cages. Ever since I was very small, I could spend hours watching them flying about and shucking the peanuts I threw at them, always with the same concentration.

I watched a little chimpanzee whose mother was trying to delouse him and who kept escaping as soon as she loosened her grip. Jumping from branch to branch on a tree sculpted out of cement, he was chased and each time caught by his mother. The children, who came in large numbers to watch, immediately identified with the baby chimpanzee who flitted with astounding agility within his area of freedom, whose limits were set by the bars of his cage.

Next to me, an elderly lady wearing a Tyrolean hat decorated with a feather, probably the grandmother of the child she was holding firmly by the hand, seemed instead to identify with the chimp's mother. Through clenched teeth, her annoyance visible,

I could hear her saying sharply to her grandson: "Er will nicht hören, der kleine Kerl, er will nicht hören!" (That little rascal doesn't want to listen, he doesn't want to listen!), squeezing his hand so hard he didn't dare take part in the general amusement.

My attention was suddenly diverted by something going on with the gorillas. Two no-nonsense guards were holding a young girl by the arms. She was round-faced, maybe sixteen; her cheeks were bright red and she smiled at me as she was led toward the exit.

I recognized the girl: a little earlier, by the lions, she had spoken to me, and from what I had understood she'd said that it was a nice day for October.

Over by the large monkeys, from the general agitation, I gathered that she had lifted her skirt to show her buttocks to the two male gorillas who, scratching their heads, had gotten more than they'd bargained for.

I wondered what she would be accused of. Of having taken these gorillas for humans? And yet, a recent report had counted gorillas among the inhabitants of the Congo.

Ruth was amused by this story when I found her back at her place, where she was preparing dinner while waiting for me.

The bed too was awaiting us, and we were happy to climb into it together. More than a year had passed since we had learned so much about each other in the space of a few moments, this knowledge bringing us together. Intertwined, no longer speaking, our eyes were smiling and we spent a long time caressing one another. Caresses of love, caresses of tenderness. There had been no sign that my body would not obey. Ruth realized it before I did. She let her tears flow, which I covered with kisses. I looked at her body, which mine was rejecting. It was as harmonious a body as I'd ever seen. What part of me was standing in the way of my desire? What memory within my body was causing it? Ruth began to shiver before she calmed herself down. And our bodies remained that way until morning, intertwined in shared emotion. It was morning when I left the silence of the bed, withdrawing from the sweetness of her arms.

Awakened in turn, Ruth prepared the coffee. As I was cutting a few slices of dark, heavy bread, she stood behind me. She lay her head sweetly on my shoulder and her hair caressed the back of my neck, but I didn't dare turn around. Our tears would have returned and I didn't want to see them covering her face. The coffee we drank in silence did us good.

An hour later, holding hands, we walked in Berlin. We walked a great deal. Ruth wanted to show me the wall, and to see the spot on the Bernauerstrasse where a spectacular escape of fifty-seven people had occurred the Sunday before. They had dug a tunnel 145 meters long and 12 meters deep, exiting near the storefront of a building with bricked-up windows. Passing back through part of the Tiergarten, where I had seen the animals the day before, it took us more than two hours to get there. It was the first Sunday since the escape, and as a result the spot had become a pedestrian destination for the West Berliners. Several dozen people were already there, awaiting their turn to bend over the tunnel's exit. In front of us, a woman was pushing a carriage with a sleeping baby. Over their heads, I noticed the word "Kuchen" (cake) in capital letters attached to the wall of the closed shop. Near the Heidestrasse, we ate a lunch that was familiar to me: wienerschnitzel and strudel.

Ruth had also wanted to show me "Checkpoint Charlie," the checkpoint reserved for the Allies, diplomats, and foreigners, but it was already late and we headed back along the canal.

It was a difficult moment. We barely dared to speak. Our encounter had been beautiful, and we didn't want to part.

This time, I was the one taking the train, and the kiss we exchanged on the platform was tender. And painful. Like the injustice of the night from which we wanted to heal. We'll see one another again, Ruth, I promise. Here or in Paris. But we'll see one another.

19

I have a specific memory. One year, Madame Saclier, the concierge at the Cité Crussol, showed us the mail rather late in the afternoon, even though she normally gave it to us in the early morning. She was coming back from a lunch that had followed the burial of Mr. Saclier, her husband.

"Now I'm like you, ma'am," she had told my mother. "That's the second one I've buried."

This memory brought to mind another, older one, which I have trouble situating in the past. It concerns one of Alex's obsessions. He was obsessed with the idea that Mother would return home one day with another man. He called him "the third man," like the film by Orson Welles. His logic, which to his mind was irrefutable, was the following: Mother had married a man, my father, and they had had a child, me, and that man had died when I was two years old. Then she had married another man, his father. And that man had also died when his son, Alex, was also two years old. So with a third it would have to be the same. Together they would have a son. After which, when the son was two years old, his father, Mother's third husband, would inevitably die a violent death.

And this little brother (because it could only be a boy) would not remember his father either. For Alex, it was unbearable.

He opened up about this obsession one night when Mother was at her choir, a troubling absence for him which prompted him to talk. I think I spoke in a calm voice. I told him that he shouldn't worry. That Mother was happy just the way things were, with her two boys.

At that time, I still didn't know about the photographs kept in that special shoe box. That night, I think we would have looked at them together, comfortably seated at the table with the photographs laid out before us. We would have tried to understand all that they told us. I would have shown him the photo in which the two friends, his father and my father, sitting on the grass, gazed at the woman they loved, who was taking their picture. And that woman was our mother.

I have since opened that box full of photographs discovered after the screening of *Jules and Jim* many times. One photograph intrigues me. The one of my grandfather with his striped cap and his yellow star sewn on the right side of his chest. What intrigued me was that the star was sewn on his right side whereas I have since learned that Jews were forced to wear it on their left. For Poland's Jews, who were far more numerous, were the orders different than for Jews in the rest of Europe?

It was a photograph of Fats Waller that I saw on the cover of a magazine called *Jazz Hot* that provided what might be an answer. The breast pocket, from which a pocket handkerchief elegantly emerges, was on the right side of Fats Waller's vest and the buttons were sewn on the left side rather than the right. I concluded that for reasons to do with the layout, the photo had been printed backward. That is probably what happened to the photograph of my grandfather, for some unknown reason. If you pay enough attention, each detail in a photograph becomes important.

Although I looked at these photographs only sporadically, they reminded me each time of that Saturday when I met Odile, next to the hundreds of images scattered pell-mell. And it always pained me to think of those abandoned images, fading from life, separated from those they represented, banished from the memories of those who should have been their keepers, washed up on the sidewalks of Saint-Ouen.

Affective memory. Involuntary memory. I was prey to memories I thought I had forgotten. Wherever I turned, they called to one another. They infiltrate where there's an opening and reappear. And at the same time, I know that try as I might, as much as I might wish not to lose them, not every moment will come back. Returning in fragments, sometimes in shreds, there will always be some moments to which I won't have access.

In the immediacy of what surrounds me today, in the disorder of events as they appear to me, not everything I find and that interests me belongs to my story.

In plunging into the past of others, will I discover something about my own? I don't know. So I do as Robert Giraud does, wandering among the memories that others provide. They keep him company, as they do me. I pass by Chez Victor periodically, where I learned to play Belote, a card game for four people. I walk the length of the Rue Oberkampf, which has become my attic. I too have learned to chat with it, to ask it good questions. Sometimes, it answers me. At one end is the neighborhood of foundry workers. One day, they will belong to history. In the meantime, at the cocktail hour, you can find them at the Vins-charbons pool hall, at 109. You can say this for them: they exist. That too is the way of the world.

Laura returned from New York, where she had spent a few months. She told me on the phone that she had something for me. I suggested having lunch at Chez Nadine, where we sometimes met. She thought it was too noisy. We met instead at a quiet Greek restaurant at the bottom of Les Gobelins.

Our conversations always began with a slightly painful silence. Laura knew this. Which is why she was always the one to start talking first. Generalities initially. And then who we've seen. "Have you heard from Robert?" No, I hadn't heard from Robert. She had sent him a postcard from New York, just as she had sent one to me. The one I received had a picture of Joan Fontaine, the star of *Letter from an Unknown Woman*.

Memories, like names and faces, reappeared then disappeared again. Laura spoke to me about New York. About what prompted her to stay so long. She had gone there in order to set up a kind of structure for visiting orchestras, in particular orchestras that play baroque music—reputed to be the most fragile—in concert halls or in the framework of certain festivals.

What had led her to such an undertaking? Music? Yes, music, of course. But especially concerts. "I like the idea of organizing the kinds of concerts I'd like to attend. And I like meeting new people. And the kinds of trips that enable me to meet them."

In New York, she had attended a concert by Bob Dylan. She was so impressed she bought all his records. She wanted to give me one of them: "Blowin' in the Wind." She asked me to listen to it closely. "I listen to it every day," she said.

"How many roads must a man walk down / Before they call him a man?" The answer to this is "blowin' in the wind." And because each answer evokes other questions, the song ends like this:

How many times must a man look up
Before he can see the sky?
Yes how many years must one man have
Before he can hear people cry?
Yes how many deaths will it take till he knows
That too many people have died?
The answer, my friend, is blowin' in the wind
The answer is blowin' in the wind.

"How many tears must a man have cried before writing such a song?" Laura asked, handing me the record.

20

Today I am going back to Poland. Back to Poland without ever having been there before. I'm on the bus that takes you from Krakow to Auschwitz.

Some twenty of us left very early this morning from Paris. There is little conversation. It's a journey that renders you mute.

A sign with an arrow: Oswiecim (Auschwitz in Polish) indicates that we will arrive shortly.

In Birkenau, near the Judenrampe, where the visit begins, a guide awaits us. She is still young, barely thirty years old. Over the course of the day she tells me that she has a degree in literature. She chose to be a guide here at Auschwitz, she tells me, in order to try to understand. Even though she thinks you can never understand everything, she adds. But she is learning. She reads what there is to read. But most of all she learns from the faces of the survivors. They are the only ones who know—here she seems to be thinking out loud—we can never really know.

I don't know who the other people are who are on the visit with me. Two women have been holding hands since we got off the bus. One of them, the older-seeming one, is still holding a suitcase she's been carrying since Paris. I make the acquaintance of the younger one. They are sisters.

"My sister wanted to show me this camp, where she was deported. So she's trying to explain it to me. But it's difficult."

"But the suitcase? Why the suitcase?"

"It's full of sweaters. Marceline was so cold last night, before we left, that she filled a suitcase with sweaters."

We walk a lot. We walk on the traces of what was. Of those who were.

There are still the ruins of the gas chambers and the crematoria, destroyed, dynamited by the murderers so that no trace, no vestige would remain to bear witness to the extermination.

A visit to the "sanitation block" through which deportees would pass upon arrival, abandoning possessions and clothing. Hair shaved. Tattooed. Striped outfit. The place where in a few hours a Jew went from a human being to a number.

And at the entrance to the Auschwitz camp, the slogan: ARBEIT MACHT FREI.

And the dormitories turned into a museum.

And in the showcases, the canisters of Zyklon B.

The hair. Tons of hair. The crutches, the wooden legs. Thousands of them. Enamel pots, kitchen utensils, brushes, and boxes of wax (brought by people who left home thinking they would be living and working elsewhere). More than a million pairs of shoes on each side of a long corridor. And apart from the others, the children's shoes. A mountain. And a mountain of eyeglasses. (Behind each pair of glasses was a life, the guide tells us.) Further along, suitcases. How many thousands of suitcases? There, the visitors slow down. Some stop. On each suitcase is painted a name. And the heads lean in. Looking left and right in the hope of finding a name: that of a relative.

"That's the day I fear the most," says the guide as we exit the building, "when a child or a parent will be unable to bring himself to leave the building, thinking he has recognized the name on a suitcase."

I knew I wouldn't have to face such a situation. The writing on one suitcase nonetheless caught my attention: "Maria Kafka Prag. XIII 833." Who was this Maria Kafka?

Then there were other collections. Documents, photographs, also bearing witness to the annihilation. Photographs that the deported carried on them at the moment of their arrest. Marriage photos, family photos, identity photos, photos of rabbis, of religious men with prayer shawls on their shoulders, photos of children on holiday or at school. I didn't catch the number of the area devoted to those coming from France where they naturally took us first. I didn't hear what the guide was saying. There, before me, was the photograph of my father. The one that was familiar to me and which I had always seen in its brown leather frame sitting on the sideboard of our dining room. In this photo, which was considerably enlarged, my father had returned to his dimensions as a man. Here we are, together, standing next to one another, face to face, both of us still. We are the same age. He is smiling at me.